"*Gabriel Hart is a real one, a journ*
don't necessarily want to go so no on
trader who doesn't take the onus to
impersonally as he pulls from a provenance that je...
in common revelation. With feral instincts, he writes from a place of
panic. Illiterate panic dovetailing into language headlong, panic as the
primal expression prolapsing into an intelligible sense where it commits
itself to posterity crystallized, a voice inspirited with the urgency and
stakes of a hail mary from the ropes. You'll be hearing it long after
you're tuckered out from reading, that rapt aura that follows you home
from a night of raging, the elusive, fragmentary truth that leaves an
exit wound. Hart renders with unforgiving clarity the personal
deliriums humans step to when they have nothing to lose, with majestic
compassion, ear for desperate colloquy, and the chutzpah to diagnose
folly as the bitter fruit of unconditional hope, distorted through
structural and stylistic abandon unafraid of crudity and tropes. Hart
embraces unusual textures lesser hands won't touch with joy and care.
A pulp stylist with disarming romantic conviction. I feel profoundly
good about literature since discovering him."

— **Manuel Marrero**, founder of expat press
and author of *Not Yet*

"*Hart continues to upend assumptions... demanding readers to*
scrutinize their expectations and understanding of the noir form."
— **Razorcake Magazine**

"*Hart's ear for rhythm is evident... He's skilled at displaying*
internal views through lyrical prose."
— **EconoClash Review**

Also by Gabriel Hart

◆

Fallout From Our Asphalt Hell

by Gabriel Hart

Close To The Bone Publishing

Close To The Bone
an imprint of Gritfiction Ltd
Rugby
Warwickshire
CV21
www.close2thebone.co.uk

Cover Design by Oliver Wheeler
and Interior Design by Craig Douglas

First Printing, 2021

Contents

◆

Introduction

I released my debut novel *Virgins in Reverse / The Intrusion* in 2018 before I had any short stories published. While the book's decade-long path to birth was fraught with false-starts, learning curves and publishing mind-fuckery, I maintain that for me, it's still easier to write a novel than it is a short story. It was sort of an arrogant, backwards move coming out of the gates like that without proving myself in short form first, but I felt I just had too much to say and I assumed tomorrow wasn't guaranteed the way I was living. Or writing, for that matter – sending what should have been a simple email was always an elaborate, cringingly-verbose, ultra-regressive, no-stone-even-asked-to-be-unturned electro-vomit communique with everything to prove. In fact, I proved I was so magical that I could clear a room (or someone's office) without physically even being there.

But once I grasped the occult knowledge of economy, I found myself challenged in new ways I assumed I was light years past. When I started flexing my short story muscle, I found I had so much to learn with compressing ideas, getting rid of unnecessary words, and reigning in my high concepts so the reader could actually sit still to focus on what should be a brief investment of their time.

So, here's twenty of my bravest attempts of brevity thus far. Most of these were written in 2020, a particularly fruitful year for me since I was on Disability with nothing but time and healing on my hands.

But just when you thought you might be off the hook with some quick reading, I've got some explaining to do.

Straight to the Bone was an instance of breakneck expedience I wouldn't recommend to anyone. I researched, wrote, edited, and submitted the story all within three hours, then was accepted to Black Hare Press's *Twenty-Twenty* Anthology by midnight that same night. I was in rare manic form that evening and today I believe it was sheer luck that it worked in my favor. *Never* submit a story the same day you wrote it, even if it somehow worked for this grizzly, gristly murder-monopoly period piece.

The Distant Prince was a story brewing in my guilty mind for years, finally given a home in the early days of Space Cowboy's *Simultaneous Times* podcast – the racy 'adult' episode, to be exact. Acknowledging a personal run of infidelity – both as victim then as arrogant perpetrator – I wrote this story as a solemn swear to myself never to lie again. To my knowledge, it has worked.

Death is smeared all over this collection – not as a way to shock but rather to *process* shock. As long as I've been writing death-obsessed songs, most end up becoming just another tombstone; where with fiction I find I actually gain some new perspectives. When my dear friend Nam took her own life in 2017, I was devastated in a way I couldn't put into words, but I wrote *Spun Pendulum* over a period of time following her exit. I found it was the only way I could express myself; to fictionalize something so painful and permanent in the form of a nihilistic police procedural. Whatever gets you through the night, I guess. With some gracious restructuring it was published online by *Bristol Noir* in September 2020.

In 2019 I was asked to facilitate a writing class for Mil-Tree, a local non-profit aimed at Vets and Active-Duty Military to heal the wounds of war. It was nothing like I expected, but better than I anticipated. I was under the impression I was going lead these men through some kind of battle-torn exorcism through the written word – something I wouldn't have been qualified for anyway. Turns out these guys already knew how to write, but war was the last thing they wanted to write about. Who could blame them? *Church of War* is sort of poking fun at my expectations, getting humbled by the mere thought of the darkness these guys had experienced, after years of assuming I had been through Hell; since it was all by my own spoiled hands it would never even compare. *Shotgun Honey* published it online in May 2020.

As a reoccurring contributor to *Simultaneous Times* sci-fi/speculative fiction podcast, *Black Pit Blues* aired in March of 2020. Looking back, it looks very Steven King to me: a tortured writer in and out of therapy whose demons either become his undoing, or he's the victim of perfectly synched self-fulfilling prophesies as dictated by nature just doing its thing. But the frightening element of this story is its non-fiction plot device – SuperPitWolves are a real phenomenon. During the time I wrote it, they were naturally breeding/evolving in the desert just ten miles from me at Whitewater Preserve.

The brief 80s/90s Los Angeles hybrid cowpunk/glam scene has always captured my imagination – I had my own cowpunk band The Starvations that was a contemporary (for our era, 1995-2005) update to that style. *The Gutter Runs Internally* is an ultra-specific speculative period piece, when that outlaw punk scene was flourishing the same time gangster rap scene was spreading. I thought: *What if the cowpunk bands took their own outlaw image to the next level, carrying real guns like gangster rappers, blurring those lines between identity and real danger?* I found out shortly after I wrote the story that members of bands like Tex and The Horseheads actually *did* pack real heat, as scoring/dealing would prove as dangerous as you would imagine. The story was graciously picked up by 10th Rule Books for their anthology "It's So Easy": Horror/Noir Inspired by Guns and Roses.

I originally wrote *Wino's Shadow* to submit to Pulp

Modern's 2011-themed issue, but Alec felt it was too literary for his genre enthusiast journal. Regardless, I was grateful for the prompt, as I got to take my love for Amy Winehouse to a desperate drag-noir corner of Hollywood. The story was immediately rescued by the brilliant Ted Prokash at Joyless House Spring 2021.

I somehow had to move all the way to the desert to start writing screenplays and treatments for an L.A. director who had also relocated here. In my brainstorming sessions for him, I reimaged Hell located on the Sun, a concept we turned into a short-film treatment, like *The Seventh Seal* meets Kenneth Anger. But I couldn't let the whole Hell as the Sun thing rest – so I wrote *Bottom's Up* for my own hustle, graciously ending up online at Pulp Modern Flash in August 2020.

The Space Between Two and Three is a tribute to my dearly departed friend Jackie Lechner, with whom I had an absolutely vivid beyond the grave/stars visit a week after her funeral, with the assistance of psylocibin. You don't have to believe me, but Manny at Expat Press saw it was substantial enough to publish online in April 2021. I performed it at Misery Loves Company the same month with help from my KORG MS-20 to depict the droning dialogue.

Dear Diana Ranswell (Mom) is pure epistolary – a letter a parent hopes they'll never receive. It chronicles a type of couple we see vacationing at Bear Creek who are ignorant to the inherent dangers of the landscape. But the poor girl finds out too late that the most localized menace was her own boyfriend. It's one of the stories that's so graphic I almost feel bad I wrote it, but when you're in the right mood it might seem fucking hilarious. Extremely over the top – but what would you do, Mom? It was an honor to add to the ever-expanding township at Bear Creek Gazette with this piece in March 2021.

When Florida's Mannison Press included *Wrath Child's Atrophy* in their *Little Boy Lost* anthology, I described it as "Stand by Me but with heavy metal kids." The Midwest was my muse for this one, along with that weird time growing up where you really leaned into metal because you had yet to discover punk. The time where you're obsessed with Satanism but had no idea what it really meant (or how meaningless it really is). The time where you only had the older teenagers to learn from, yet to a fault since they seemed to be punching it a little too hard.

Keeping up with the kids, *BAPTISM!* is another grim study of children's behavioral patterns – specifically, the difference between what boys define as fun, opposed to girls. Is violence learned or is it biological? This was originally published in the 2018 *Desert Writer's Guild Anthology.*

Kept Change will likely be the most controversial story in here, but it's never my intention to shock the reader, much less make any grand gender-politic statement as a straight white male. Yet, I felt pregnant enough with an idea to explore both the sacred nature and reactionary nonsense of the transgender phenomenon, reimagined in a more dystopian setting as a safe space to do so. For the record, I am one hundred percent on the side of transgender rights, yet I acknowledge how far removed I am, therefore I have a long way to go to fully understand it. But with that comes a sincere fascination and respect for the courage it requires. As someone who loved cross-dressing for a time, I did it as a sort of tribute to women, embracing the elegance while being very comfortable in my own body. But I realized how ridiculous, even insulting this might be to a real trans person, who are in sincere identity struggle as opposed to my Ed Woodian whimsy. My main crux of the story: if people comfortably switched genders *en masse*, would we maintain our eternal War of the Sexes? Would the fresh males double-down on their newfound machismo, the transitioned women eventually feeling trapped in their roles as a result? I'd like to think there would be a more spiritual integration, a transcendence of gender, an all-is-one evolution like Genesis P. Orridge theorized. Regardless, it's exciting to witness such a severe societal shift, wherever it may lead; so long as its culture doesn't get co-opted by corporate opportunism. It's understandable why this story was rejected by three different venues, but also logical that Expat Press ended up publishing it online in August 2020.

I'll never forget the night I had a house guest over, when they pointed at my triangular graph outline for *Process of Elimination* laying on my coffee table and wondered if I was planning a hit out on someone. Then, I got sort of paranoid anyway – *do I really give off that vibe?* "I was simply trying to fit a potential novel's worth of material into 500 words as an exercise, and it required a lot of money math and pyramid-scheming, so settle down and let me fix you a drink."

Closed for Take-Out was the one pandemic story I allowed myself to write in 2020 – it was published online by Bristol Noir that September. One of the wildest things I witnessed wasn't people hoarding toilet paper – it was the lines around the block at local gun shops, when we assumed it was the end of the world and might have to defend our properties. I added some melodrama to balance the real-time panic, but as I write this the virus is still wrecking absolute havoc, and our future remains uncertain.

In 2016, I had the honor of my piece *The Visitor* included in Dutch artist Van Rijn's book *In the Woods and On the Heath*, appearing alongside his erotic pen and ink masterpieces amongst other passages by Aleister Crowley, Paul Eluard, Luis Aragon and other purveyors of the profane. The book remains one of my prized possessions – I wish I could show you how beautiful it is. The Visitor chronicles the type of insanity being madly in love (and lust) can bring, where you feel the whole world is speaking to you, entitling you to do whatever you damn well please, for better or worse.

A much shorter version of *Artificial Midnight* was scrawled over a decade ago. It was haphazardly, drunkenly acted out by me and some close friends as a makeshift radio drama on L.A.'s Kill Radio. I forgot about it until I went through one of the worst – and potentially dangerous – breakups of my life. I found myself relating so much to the suffocation of the story, that I fleshed it out further to cope with the lingering emotional damage. Thank God it's finally seeing the light of day here, in your hands instead of mine – never have I wanted a story to get as far away from me as possible.

I think it does a disservice to a dream when you try explaining it in traditional narrative. The fragmented, semi-experimental dread of *The All-The-Way House* takes you through an insidious reoccurring dream I still have at least once a month. I swear I've never seen this house in real life before, yet by now I know every room with such chilling familiarity. My theory is that it's a purgatorial form of the punkhouse my friends and I grew up at, and every time I return there in my dreams, it offers a retroactive warning of what else might be lingering if we never left. But this "story" seemed too strange for any of my usual genre-fiction venues, until I reminded myself what a unique corner Expat Press continues to carve out – they published it online the week of Halloween in 2020.

It's shameful to confess just how non-fiction *The Lonesome Defeat of Bridge Repair* is, but no one really needs to know that. It was originally published in the *Bleeding Heart and Burning Love* anthology by Things in the Well (Australia), then reprinted online by Bristol Noir in December 2020 where it turned the stomachs of a whole new audience.

We end this collection with a never-before published novelette-length crime/sci-fi/dystopian/horror story, *Skattertown*. I wrote this one under the influence of copious Irish coffee for adrenalized abandon; to ponder how far society might go for the perfect drug for our imperfect times. I don't think I can recall a writing session feeling like a party more than this one.

Oh, and if it hasn't already clicked, the title I chose for this collection *Fallout from Our Asphalt Hell* is a double, almost triple entendre. We know "fallout" mostly in the nuclear sense – the radioactive particles carried into the atmosphere after an explosion or accident that gradually fall back as dust or precipitation; we often refer to it as the adverse side-effects or results of any situation, really. So, I see these stories as a sort of collateral damage, just as much as I see the act of *reading* these stories as your way of temporarily "falling-out" of the real-time nightmare we've created. Given the extreme nature of the pieces herein, after you're through, you might even return to reality somewhat relieved, like maybe it wasn't as bad as you remembered? That might sound presumptuous, but then again none of these stories would exist if it weren't for all those big maybes...

Gabriel Hart
Morongo Valley, CA

Fallout From Our Asphalt Hell

Straight to the Bone

It was 9:30pm when Jacob Schick jumped, startled by a fierce knuckle-rap at his office door – Magazine Repeating Razor Company in Stanford, Connecticut. Working overtime after his employees left for the day, he was over-caffeinated, thin-nerved. Putting the finishing touches on his big deal with American Chain and Cable Company, it would be the most lucrative contract he'd sign in his life. Whoever it was at the door, he was already sure it was the last thing he needed.

Before he could react, they knocked again.

Harder.

Louder.

His chest tightened as he walked to the door, shaking his head.

He opened the door to three men who looked more upset than he was. The one in the middle wore a strapped-tight German leather trench coat under his black Fedora, which he lifted up to reveal his piercing gaze. The two flanking him wore black slacks, white button-ups, their ties at half-mast.

"Can I help you?"

"We shall see how this goes," said the German. "My name is Johan Henckels, heir to the Zwilling J.A. Henckels company. As you know, we are the makers of the world's finest straight-razor."

"Ah ha, that's great!" said Schick, his mood lightening. He assumed this was no more than a poorly timed international elbow rub to talk shop, so he perked up professional. *Germans and their wacky time-zones,* he thought.

"Would you like to..."

Before he could invite them inside, the three pushed

past him.

"Mr. Schick, these are my American colleagues from Proctor & Gamble who make many fine products. For this visit, I will note they provide the best quality shaving creams, soaps, and badger-hair shaving brushes."

Schick reached out his hand to shake. The two men nodded, hands remaining in their pockets as they rocked back and forth on their loafers, impatient.

"All right, gentlemen. Great to have you here. What is it I could do for you?"

"Mr. Schick, first of all, we are concerned," said Johan. "Concerned that you are making men... soft."

"Soft?"

"Yes, your magazine razor patent. It was unfortunate enough for our company when the safety razor was introduced, but at least men were still at one with the blade when changing them out. While I admire the fact that you were once a Colonel and your magazine strip blade replacements resemble a clip for a classic repeater rifle, the problem is that men don't get to handle the blades anymore. Not only has it hurt my company, but you have helped erase a vital part of masculinity in our morning ritual."

"Sure, well... it's a lot safer. No more getting cut, that's why is became so popular."

"Yes, but you are making men scared of their own grooming tool. In addition, you've grown so arrogant by the success of your product that you are going a step further. We understand that you are about to forge a substantial deal with American Chain & Cable?"

"Correct, to patent the world's first electric razor!" he said, beaming. "I can show you the prototype right over at my desk..."

"That will be unnecessary, Mr. Schick. Now, we also understand that while it's electric, it is also being called a 'dry razor.""

"That's right," said Jacob. "No more..."

He looked at Mr. Proctor & Gamble.

"...soap or brushes to get in the way."

His speech nose-dived.

"Aha, you're starting to understand why we are here," said Johan. "Mr. Schick, while I commend you on your invention, I'd like you to think very hard about what that means for the future of our companies."

Jacob could feel his pores giving hard birth to cold sweat.

"I... I'm not really sure what to say."

"Have any contracts been signed yet?"

"No, that's all happening tomorrow."

"Oh, good. So, we still have a chance," said Johan, finally cracking a smile.

"A chance for what?"

He hadn't noticed the Proctor & Gamble at his sides until they grabbed both his wrists, holding them behind him like a downhill skier.

"What?!? I..."

"Mr. Schick, when was the last time you had a real blade against your skin?"

"I... I... I don't know, I..."

"I'll take that as so long you can't recall."

Johan pulled out his own personal Henckels Solingen blade from the inner pocket of his jacket. He slowly put it to Jacob's straining neck.

"You see, the thing with an electric razor, is that they serve only one purpose – shaving. And not very well. Is it true that the electric razors will actually *stimulate* hair growth, as it cuts just above the surface of the skin? Like right about here, like this?"

Johan hovered the blade, barely touching his flesh,

so it just skimmed the flecks of his incoming growth. Jacob's whole body shivered as he tried to scream through their hands over his mouth.

"Well, sometimes the old ways are the best ways, Mr. Schiff. The way the straight razor gets the closest shave..."

He pressed the blade into his bulging jugular, his flesh pillowing around the metal.

"... getting right in there, deep... to the real root of the problem!"

He swiped diagonal, unzipping his skin to a crimson-flood. Then, the same slash of pre-emptive vengeance on his left, the rip briefly interrupted by Schick's collarbone before he gouged it back in for a third. His life ran down his neck, now both sides in a heavy, pulsing deluge. Their hands remained over his screaming mouth to muffle his protests, following him all the way down to the floor. His eyes grew wider until the pleading ceased.

"I think there is a bathroom down the hall we can use," said Johan, pointing the way out of the office to his two accomplices.

They closed the office door behind them. They walked the hall. They entered the bathroom. They turned on the hot water. One of them pulled out a bar of Proctor & Gamble Ivory Soap. The other presented a shaving brush, which would be perfect for getting deep under their fingernails.

The Distant Prince

A lie is told – not just to protect our own selfish agendas, but often to keep someone else's feelings from being hurt. We fool ourselves to believe that the latter is less harmful, yet either way we are engaging in black magic, the antithesis of The Gods, creating an alternate reality that will have no natural fusion, no magnetic force of nature… These lost, fickle fragments of anti-life we create will float as debris in our inner space, jumbling up our frequencies as we become more preoccupied with their impossible maintenance than we are with our own daily evolutions. If enough of these 'abortions of The Soul' are rendered, they will fuse into a panorama of blindness within us; whose foundation one cannot actually see, but will be the only solid ground left for us to stand on, as reality as we once knew it will then begin to fade from view…

"Jim, honey… what's the matter… What happened?!?!"
He dismounted her with a jolt, much faster than their passion had initially conjoined their loins. He recoiled to the corner, palms in face. His blue-balled panting muffled through his fingers like he was suffocating himself. He said nothing.

"Jim! What the fuck is wrong with you, honey?" her voice teetering from sympathy to condemnation.

"I'm. I'm… I'm fine, it's ok, Shelly," he lied.

"Uh, no! It's not ok, obviously! You were just fucking my brains out right perfect and now you're in the corner like a dunce and you're… shaking? What the hell, Jim?" she shriek-whispered. "Honestly, you're making me feel like I'm an open sore right now!"

Tongue-tied, he saw the moon beaming on her face through their curtains to a slightly altered angle since she sat up. Now it was giving her face a hideous, malevolent quality – a far cry from the young angel he had just been making sincere love to. A young angel that caused him to jump out of her.

"Really, I promise everything is okay. I'm really sorry, baby." he said, revealing nothing. He was more concerned with covering his manhood, quickly devolving into modesty as he wondered what just happened. After all, how could he explain to her what was wrong if he didn't know what had just occurred?

Jim thought quick as he made himself get up and crawl back into bed with his sweetheart of almost three years. He knew exactly what he saw, but opted for more ambiguity, as the truth would have simply locked him out of her heart. He salvaged some confidence, whispering to her as he pulled up the sheets again, steering it gingerly back into the safe, romantic cul-de-sac that he was doing donuts in just minutes earlier.

"I think I got so deep with you that I got a little dizzy and I thought I was going to pass out." He was getting quite good at lying after a year of erratic infidelity.

Shelly's mood changed dramatically, a smile spilling across her face. "Good answer!" she sighed. She handed him a glass of water from the nightstand, like a dutiful cheerleader to her marathon man. She seemed appeased, curled up into him, her softness contouring into his stiff oblivion.

It was only 8:46pm. Though they had been in the throes of passion for almost an hour, it was enough for Shelly to fall into a light sleep, slightly snoring every so often. Jim lay facing away, unable to relax as he gazed into the taunting digital marquee of their alarm clock. *What time was it, anyway?* The numbers on the clock appeared foreign as hieroglyphics, mere primitive symbols compared to what he had actually just seen.

He had seen the other woman in her. No, he didn't *see* the other woman *in* her – her face had actually *become* the other woman's face.

He looked away.
Looked back.
Still there.
Blinked.
Still there.
Thrusted harder.
Still there.

Gazed into her eyes, more presence. It was still the other woman. It had been months ago. Nobody except him and the other woman knew. Shelly would have never known about it, had she not just somehow *become* her.

He turned his head to make sure she was still fast asleep. He rose to open the window. It was sweltering – he needed some cold air to sober up his own guilt-ridden insanity. He took the two steps towards the pane, gently lifted the latch, pushed up the window frame. He looked at the moon, blinding in its luminescence, yet it took on a shade and shape he never recalled seeing. There it sat, cradled in the clearest of brisk night skies – a dull matte grey finish covering any of its normal texture or definition. A superimposition. Directly in the center was a small but undeniable black blemish, a feature never seen before on this most ubiquitous feature of night. He was sure he wasn't hallucinating, but transfixed on what seemed like a honest-to-God glitch in permanence. He wondered how something so colorless and bereft of life could be such a taunting presence. *Was it actually present?*

He returned to the bed, defeated, confused, fatigued. His elusive paranoia finally wore him out and he fell into a dull sleep.

Jim, her marathon man.

He awoke gently to a familiar embrace at 2:15am, her thumb and forefinger tracing the contours of his slowly stiffening cock. "I'm not done with you yet…" she playfully whispered into his ear, as he melted into her nocturnal advance. He took his arm under her neck as he explored her underworld with his other hand, assuring the arousal was mutual before he threw his leg over, plunging into her with abandon, yet focused gusto.

As if his whole lie depended on it.

Steadily, his confidence rose with each thrust into her. The bed lamp still off, it was the moon that cast the only sabers of light into the room, spilling onto Shelly's face, grimacing with pleasure, pain, everything beyond and in between. Her face shown bright like a spotlight presentation, something he wasn't prepared for the second time, the evening's sole source of illumination gradually altering her features once again like the shadows of a sundial.

This time, Jim did not recoil. Instead, he was re-animated in his wee-hour exhaustion as he gorged himself into Shelly. His oil-drill rhythms quickened, his lengths deepening, muscles tightening as he hungrily indulged this time in his preferred future, into a face that was not hers. He uttered the unthinkable.

"I love you."

It was Shelly's turn to recoil. She half-giggled nervously before surrendering to the hour's previous bewilderment, wiggling out from under him and sitting upright.

"Jim, what is going on? You can't blame me for being shocked to hear you say that… You haven't said those words to me in years now. Maybe I've become some callous bitch but now you're acting strange. Even though you're trying to be sweet. Just give it up already, please?"

He rose off his knees and planted his feet onto the floor, saying not a word, save the residual panting of his deflating passion. He looked toward the window, then moved towards it in slow-motion, catatonic with stoic curiosity, possessed by what he saw in the sky. Jim reclaimed his spot at the sill, looking up. The blemish on the moon had grown larger, as did the rest of the grey sphere around it. Now it resembled a giant eye, with odd detail in the pupil that felt familiar.

Transfixed on the orb, it wasn't long before its dull grey appearance began to blur and swirl into a far more disturbing image, as grey turned to blue, and continents began to form on the surface, slightly obscured by slivers of white like those of a cataract.

It was his worst nightmare – the planet Earth, slowly fading away; as he looked around, he was no longer in his own home, but in the barren landscape of this moon he had made for himself, his own anti-world constructed by lies kept under such pressure they had finally solidified into his own private rocky foundation. After years of not being present, he would no longer be allowed to see what was always right in front of him.

Spun Pendulum

She stuck the note into her cleavage so they wouldn't search the apartment any more than they would need to. It would all be right there. Blatant. Hopeless to argue over. Impossible to look away from. She wanted to make a statement, not a mystery.

"… as a three-year old orphan left on the streets of Korea, I was found by my foster parents and taken in. We moved to America when I was five, and while I was given a good life, that void of being left on the streets by my real parents was one I could never reconcile, like an itch I could never scratch.

Since I wasn't born here, I've had to reapply for citizenship every couple years, some updated terrorist-paranoia shit from 9/11. And guess what? They fucking denied me this time, all because of that time I beat my boyfriend with my high heel. He fucking deserved it. I didn't deserve this.

And now that this fucking shithead is in office, they told me I'm going to be deported back to Korea, and if I didn't turn myself in within three days, they'd come to my apartment. Well, this is fucking day three. Come find me, bitches!

And then my boyfriend won't leave his wife. I mean, what would you do? Your parents didn't want you, your boyfriend doesn't want you, and now your own fucking country doesn't want you?

Maybe the Land of Milk and Honey is this way, right here.
KIM

They identified themselves as Officer Ramos and Deputy Johnson, speaking from the hallway through her locked door. Sympathetic, though firm.

"Are you armed or any sort of any danger to

yourself, or anyone else?"

Silence.

Then, a tiny yap of what sounded like a small dog.

Ramos gave Johnson *the look* as he grabbed the battering ram, as Johnson got behind it for extra weight. Four heartfelt heaves to splinter the door enough to kick the panel in.

Through the hole they could see a little Yorkie going apeshit, unaware of its own diminutive form. Ramos reached through to unlock the knob, clinching eyes with Johnson once more as he pushed it wide open.

While it was still early evening, they were just too late. The limp body of a tiny but gorgeous Korean woman hung from the ceiling fan, a dog collar choking her neck in permanence. The leash attached was coiled up tight like twisted wrought iron. As the leash reached maximum tautness, she began to slowly rotate the other direction, implying she still possessed a post-mortem form of perpetual motion. A barstool stood two feet away from her dangling high heels, still rocking in that slight, slow pendulum, indicating the freshness of her death. Both stilettos pointed to where she should have remained standing in a better world. Her body subtly spun like a ballerina music box, or a cake in a display window, allowing a witness to be privy to every detail whether they wanted to or not.

They wanted to. While Johnson trembled with glazed chickenshit apprehension, Ramos led them in. Johnson trailed cautiously behind him. He knew it was against protocol but couldn't help crouching down to try petting the puppy back to tranquility.

Ramos drew his gun, aiming at everything in calculated scans, though no one else was accompanying the swinger. They both froze once their eyes adjusted to the dim of the apartment, bringing her outfit into focus: a black leotard over white tights into a couple of *very* expensive heels – her take on a Playboy Bunny get-up, minus the ears.

Johnson stood there staring paralytic. His mouth agape, never had a man with a gun firmly in his hand been so disarmed. He took a knee, now clearly genuflecting rather than studying, with only the urge to return her silence with his own. He started to sob uncontrollably.

"The fuck are you doing, Johnson? You wanna be of real help to this shitshow and do your fucking job by any chance?" Ramos had surveyed half the room before he saw his young partner, enchanted and unprofessional.

"Sorry, man. This is just my first time seeing something like this. I didn't realize someone could do themselves in like this and look so... I hate to fucking say it, but *at peace*?" Johnson's voice quivered then broke into tears again, immediately emasculating himself.

"Why are you fucking crying?!?" Ramos was mystified as well, but only at his partner's pathetic reaction. It made him squirm in shame. He knew Johnson was a little unstable, but he was his brother-in-law now, so this was also becoming an emotional conflict of interest.

He thought of his sister, Johnson's new wife, and did his best to cool his jets. Begrudgingly, he walked over to indulge his partner's divergent observations, before shaking his head.

"Listen, I know it's a little weird when they're dead and still have their eyes open, but it's nothing to psychoanalyze. Some fools just have a braver gaze into the abyss, is all."

Johnson waited for his partner to resume his search of the room so he could stubbornly return to his vantage. As she tauntingly rotated, he noticed something white ensconced in her. He took a couple steps closer.

The note.

A "Dear world" letter.

"Call a detective…" Johnson slurred, a ventriloquist caught under his own tired gag.

***

It wasn't at all how it looked. Ramos assumed Kim was a prostitute with her scant, sensational get-up. But after the note was analyzed, her close friends and family were contacted – turns out that's just how she dressed while she was at home. A little eccentric, as her evening wear looked hand-picked by Hefner himself.

"She just liked to feel pretty," is what her best friend had revealed through pleading sobs as she petted her newly adopted Yorkie. After Kim's inexplicable absence from work, her phone went right to voicemail. After leaving plenty of her own footprints on Kim's door, she was the one who called the cops.

Kim's note unraveled a vast, sad state of affairs, one that indicted the country's current xenophobic administration as the last straw in her perfect storm of abandonment. Her permanent exit an incendiary battle cry of both the personal and political.

***

Monday morning cruelly found Johnson at his desk looking like another stinking corpse after a long weekend. He showed up an hour late, leaving no choice but to wait for a scolding from Ramos, adding to his skin crawling paranoid hangover. He stared out the window onto the passing traffic, searching for reasons not to run right into it.

"What the fuck happened to you, Johnson? We

were trying to call you all fucking weekend, and now you're an hour late here? My sister is worried sick. Have you even called her yet?"

Johnson responded by covering his face with his hands, then collapsing into his forearms on his desk. He figured the longer he remained silent, the longer it would take for Ramos to find out he was still drunk.

Ramos grimaced, lips trembling. He leered closer to Johnson as he lowered his head to sniff for the big clue.

He found it.

"You're fucking drunk? You fucking piece of shit. Eight months of sobriety down the fucking drain? What is my sister going to say? She took a chance marrying you, and I took a big chance on you joining the force even though you possessed every fucking red flag in the book..." Ramos reeled himself in with his volume, though not his spite. "You had a fucking record and I made it magically disappear for you, you son of a bitch." Ramos whispered point blank into his ear. "Am I a fucking idiot?"

Johnson looked up at Ramos, focusing on the veins in his forehead so he wouldn't have to look him in the eyes.

"No, I am. I'm sorry. I'm gone. I'll get my things."

Ramos wound up and slapped him across his grovel-face, reminding him who used to be in charge of whom.

"Give me your badge, your gun, and then go see my fucking sister, you piece of shit."

***

Johnson did not go to see his worried-sick wife. Instead, he broke his half-drunk haze with a sneer as he got into his car, turning the other way out of the station, and rolled steady towards Los Angeles Street. "What sad naïve symbolism," he thought – the histrionics of giving up his gun to Ramos when he had the one under his bed at home, and then another one in his glove compartment. He flipped it open to make sure. *There it is, right there.*

His adrenaline was nearly sobering, tightening his stomach. He realized this was really going to happen. He was actually going to do it. He made a right into the Los Angeles Dept of Immigration, where people were just doing their job. That, he was convinced, *was the fucking problem.*

He exited his vehicle, approaching the front of the building with errant strides before swinging open the glass door. Once inside, he paused in panic; a temporary thought that *this was crazy* left his mind as fast as it came. He swayed like a buoy, behind a Medusa-head of lines of people beaten down by fate, now awaiting the fist of geographical circumstance and fickle illusions of law. He prayed to God for a sign.

His DTs careened with his pining, his mourning, his suffocated, writhing projections. He saw his mistress Kim, her apparition hanging above the balding man at the 2nd window. She slowly spun like her last dance in the dark apartment where he left her. Target determined, he raised his gun and fired. Blood sprayed the shattered partition. The room choke-screamed in muffled pandemonium, as Johnson put the gun to his head, determined to finally find the peace that his honey achieved, that way, right there.

Church of War

My eyes strained to adjust to sudden nightfall. The church's cross stood silhouetted against the last-ditch rays of a gorgeous sunset; both of which I knew I didn't deserve.

Why was I volunteering for a non-profit when I was broke, two steps from destitute? I had my reasons. It was my first teaching gig, facilitating a writing class for local Vets and Active Military to help heal the wounds of war. I've never served, but I had a hole blown in my spiritually bankrupt soul that I was pouring booze into all week. All it did was sink me deeper into my own trenches. Perhaps it wasn't the most ethical choice to beeline from Happy Hour to a church, where we were gonna have group exorcism with guys who had *really* seen Hell on Earth.

But like I said, I had my reasons.

I walked in, clipping my shoulder on the door jamb. I was impressed they had all beat me there, their instilled military punctuality ahead of schedule. Until I looked at the clock on the wall and saw I was actually twenty minutes late.

I felt like a fraud, the way they all displayed their own heroic Hellscapes by regions on their Ballcaps of Honor – Korea, Vietnam, Afghanistan. Then the other Scorched Earth campaigns – Desert Storm, Operation Iraqi Freedom. I imagined the complexity of guts, glory and deception that these men represented. To be both hero and pawn for our country that couldn't keep its tongue out of a beehive.

And who was I? Some spoiled brat that could have everything going for him if he hadn't created a guilt-ridden Hell with his own two hands, that's who. But I had found my people, at least for what I came for. If anyone would understand, it would be these compromised men.

I proposed we all dig deep, exhume every ghost that woke us up at night screaming.

"Hello, my name is Bradley Miller, and I'd like to start by saying 'thank you' for your service," I said. I was met with a couple nods of acknowledgment while the others just stared a thousand miles past me.

"I'd like us to start with a prompt I've prepared. I'd like us to explore regret. What's the darkest, most remorseful thing you've experienced that you've never gotten to dissect?"

Nearly everyone communicated reluctance, if not full denouncement of the exercise. I realized I had forgotten the most important part.

"And by the way, this is all confidential. Let us pledge that none of this will leave the room. You have my word."

Mr. Vietnam was the shot-caller of this tight-knit group. He chided the others, reminding them that I was the one in charge, to do as I say. Show the kid some respect, he said.

Heads went down as pens scratched pads. I was an outsider, but grateful for this opportunity. Maybe this was all I needed to get a good night's sleep.

It was gonna be fine. I was convinced whatever these guys were going to share – war crimes, hasty decisions that cost their buddy's lives, maybe – all bound to be far worse than my one-time moral hiccup last week. Especially considering larger body counts these men have under their belts.

I was the first one finished. To give them the confidence to share, I went first.

I let it all out – what I did to the guy, where his body was now, what I did with the gun. What he did to cross me to justify the permanence of my knee-jerk vigilante justice.

But they went rogue on me.

One guy wrote about putting his dog to sleep. Another guy wrote about cheating on his wife. Another wrote about never seeing his kids and some other guy just wrote about his boring morning that day.

While Mr. Afghanistan recalled the time he nearly blew his own brains out, I saw Mr. Vietnam with his back turned, talking on his cell, urgently relaying the address of the church.

I jumped out of my seat, lunging for his phone as he swung at me, connecting with my nose.

Maybe it was Mr. Desert Storm that whacked me with his cane while I held my nose to stop bleeding, but the flashing lights made a blurring strobe before everything went black.

Black Pit Blues

As he drove home from his weekly therapy appointment, Richard's mood began to plummet.

He left the appointment on an inspired high. Evasive breakthroughs and revelations finally made clear through the applied logic inside him all along, tearing at his ribcage to be unleashed.

For a while back there, he thought he might be cured.

He let himself get too excited, too quick. Now, he witnessed his shadow forming in the dimming light of personal illumination, unable to find the tools to balance the hemispheres. His last bit of desperate logic asked: *Am I getting depressed out of nowhere simply from a reverse Pavlovian reaction to the sun setting?* Maybe it was fatigue from the long day? But as he watched our inconceivably-sized flaming ball of hot plasma disappear behind the mountains, it was clear why – now, he knew too much.

Now, he understood *too well* how it all worked – the amoral inner workings of human behavior – one insidious element withstood:

Fear.

A fear that now transcended beyond motive or phobia. A self-sufficient entity whose power lay in the ability to feed off of itself, nothing or no one to blame for its presence except its very presence. How one might attempt to describe God to an atheist.

If this feeling refused to subside, he imagined himself yearning for the Devil-may-care pre-therapy days of fear-based motivation, delusion and self-destruction, where at least he could still harness the essence of romance.

The only thing propelling him home was his dog. A

white, scrappy Jack Russell who had one of those ecstatic wind-tunnel grins. He named him Chipper after his bright disposition, whose main preoccupation was a ceaseless washing of Richard with saliva-drenched gratitude for rescuing him two months ago.

"If only human beings could be that fearless with their acknowledgments," he often thought.

Now in a slow panic, he combed his mental rolodex for every tool the therapist gave him to battle the weight of this erratic melancholy.

"At least I'll be home soon and will be allowed to stare at something other than this bleak horizon," he thought, as he traveled up Oak Glen Rd., past the city limits of Hemville to his right.

Hemville was one of those repellant anti-towns you might be accidentally born in but you'd never in your right mind move to. Beyond the one-square mile radius of dilapidated trailers and homes in various states of natural decay or probationer remodel, there was nothing there – no schooling or even businesses (legal). Luckily, you rarely saw a child forsaken enough to be born in Hemville, as its main industry was the raising of Pit Bulls for fighting. While this was the main event there, no one outside of the shit-hole town would ever witness it. The town's imposing, nefarious reputation would act as its own security wall.

What they would witness: scar-damaged Pit Bulls past their prime, barely hanging on, left on the side of Oakglen Rd. at Hemville city limits.

It dawned on him. Richard was afraid he was going to see one. He realized it was the reason this hollowed out sense hit him every time he passed Hemville. It was an empathic anger, unable to conceive why someone could just throw away a living thing. These Pit Bulls had created their own canine ghetto on this stretch of road. Too often, he would have to swerve to miss one. Unable to distinguish the borders of the road versus the shoulder, the overgrown orphans would often take over parts of both lanes, straying aimlessly like homeless in Skid Row where they saw no logic – therefore, no bounds – for their discard.

And there it was. He saw one lying on the side of the road. Richard was flash-choked, hypnotized by mortality. He prayed he could somehow unsee it. He looked in his rear view, saw the light change green about a mile down the road, unleashing another batch of rush-hour commuters. Not one for restraint, he pulled up to the dead dog in the middle of the asphalt, in futile hope the hit was recent and there may be some life left.

The second he hit the brakes the black Pit sprang to its paws. Richard had merely interrupted another rogue nap anywhere the dog's exhaustion and boredom would sluggishly dictate. His nubby tail wagged pathetically like a compromised metronome, trying to communicate: *Are you my new person?*

Richard took a knee to pet the Pit's short, moonlit shiny coat. He noticed infected areas where no hair would grow – no doubt battle-scars from the ring. He saw the pleading desperation in – he looked underneath – *his* eyes, already welling up with moisture and hope.

"Does Chipper need a friend?" he thought. Richard was constantly guilt-ridden with the time he had to leave Chipper alone at home, after his long work hours and extra mental-health obligations. If he opened his car door, he'd likely jump right in. He had a soft spot for this misunderstood breed ever since his ex's Pit showed him how sweet they could be, that it was humans who corrupted them into such aggressive, unpredictable creatures.

Which... this one would be a prime candidate for.

His shadow elongated as the headlights from the

oncoming batch of cars began to intrude on his tender moment. The one in front honked pre-maturely to warn him, in case *he* was some crazy thing that knew no difference between the road and the shoulder.

"Sorry, buddy. Can't do it. Good luck, pup!" he said, giving the Pit one more pet, waving a silent *sorry* to the traffic as he jumped back in.

Now, of course, he was stuck in traffic. *"No good deed goes unpunished,"* he thought. *"Not even an abandoned good deed."* His car crawled along, now enveloped in the slow-moving fleet of working stiffs, still working to get the hell home. The traffic had him trapped in the right lane. Richard's skull shrunk tight round his brain with the nonsensical honking that came next.

He looked behind him, throwing his arms up. "Ain't gonna make us go any faster, folks!"

What Richard didn't know is that it was the black Pit they were honking at. The dog had been following him in bumbling yet determined pursuit – jumping up on his hind legs, tapping on the back bumper with his paws any chance he got. From an outside perspective, it appeared Richard was the owner who abandoned the black Pit, trying to get away clean. No doubt the trail of cars were residents of his own Bonita Pines, the next town up full of slightly more concerned citizens in the backwoods spectrum.

One guy stopped his car, got out and banged on Richard's trunk, screaming, "Get your fucking dog!!!"

Richard gunned it, swerving onto the shoulder. He swore he heard the guy say he had *a fucking gun.*

The black Pit galloped after him, onto the shoulder then out into the road. It appeared Richard was doing that asshole thing of impatiently passing everyone. A quarter mile down from the jam, Richard slowed back down to the rural speed limit of 30 miles per hour. He decelerated further to ease his rapid heart rate, over-amped from who he thought was a road-rager threatening to kill him.

"What the fuck was that?" he said aloud. "The guy has some aversion to French fries or something?"

Richard was referring to the delicious exhaust from his veggie-oil converted Volkswagen New Beetle, which everyone thought smelled like fast food fried spuds.

Including the black Pit, who eventually followed the smell all five miles to Richard's house.

***

It was a small miracle the black Pit didn't get hit by a car during his hour-long journey. The way his coat camouflaged him into the night, making him virtually disappear into the into the zero-light pollution darkness. The way he kept his nose turned up to capture the sweet smell of whatever was cooking in that fried oil he knew was just for him.

Nose, not eyes, on the prize.

On the final stretch, his tail wagged with accelerated gusto as he zig-zagged up his final stretch, the intoxicating exhaust becoming more concentrated as Richard pulled into his driveway.

The Pit saw the lights on, welcoming him to his new home. Better yet, he saw his new person was already cooking. Something different than what he had been smelling, something better. *This was quite an exhausting little chase game*, the black Pit thought. Though he liked games, he was tired of this one and wanted to eat already.

He scratched at the front door, not wanting to bark quite yet as he was still feeling out the pack order of Richard and, *"Oh! There's another puppy! Could this get any better?"*

The scratching wasn't working, but that full-sized window in the kitchen looked like it would!

He trotted over to the glass, sitting there like a good boy until his new person would see that he was ready to eat.

Richard assumed he was having a full-psychotic break when he saw the black Pit outside his window. He dropped the full-pot of pasta and boiled water on his torso, scorching the entirety of his mid-section, crotch, and upper thighs. He screamed, blood-surging heat racing from veins to extremities. He bellowed every blue obscenity in every inflection, dumbfounded at the surreal sight at his pane.

The black Pit, which had nearly seduced him back on Oakglen Rd., turned harbinger of his own fraying stability.

Richard waddled violently to his front door, swinging it open. The shock of the cold night air hit his blistering skin as he pointed to the wayward traveler.

"Are you for real? Get out of here! Get out!"

He made sweeping gestures toward the forest with his index finger.

"I said get out of here! Git!"

The black Pit's eyes watered in disbelief at the sudden change of plans. Reluctantly, he got the message – he had heard that tone incessantly from his last person, and it only meant two things:

Cruelty.

Then, abandonment.

He lowered his head, sulking in defeat. But respecting his strange and mean new person was better than not having a new person at all.

He trotted off, disappearing into the enveloping darkness of the pines, now anything but *Bonita*.

***

While a grueling year and a half later, Richard was finally experiencing real progress at his therapy sessions. Not the deceiving kind that would last for an hour before the floor would fall from under him again. But the real permanence of gravity, where he felt his feet firmly placed on the Earth, able to take small but confident steps forward.

As someone who fancied himself a writer, he had never been so glad to run out of material. Not just his fodder at therapy, but at home in front of his taunting computer, where he was convinced everything he wrote had to be some kind of heavy, semi-autobiographical exorcism in order to be 'good.'

As part of his finishing therapy, he made a big decision to take a break from writing, to see what would happen. He grew incredibly anxious every time he wrote, his own worst critic who would never be satisfied. As much as he was getting out of his system, it had an accumulative boomerang effect that often left him feeling worse than before.

One Saturday he bravely explored the mundanity of idle time. He found an unlikely power in it that gave him an unspoken solidarity with his neighbors, their empty smiles no longer a mystery.

Maybe they were empty, because they, too, had run out of material? He thought

One thing that was full of its own material, yet unemotional and did all the thinking for you:

The morning paper.

Richard couldn't remember if he had ever done something so simple as to sit down with his morning coffee and read the damn paper.

"Let's do this," he said.

He scanned the front page of his small-town news, zeroing in on a substantial headline toward the bottom that continued on page 2:

BONITA PINES PRESERVE CLOSED DUE TO 'NEW' SUPERWOLF ATTACKS

Three local hikers were attacked on Friday afternoon by what rangers are calling a dangerous new 'hybrid' wolf breed.

The incident happened in Bonita Pines Preserve, the protected area of wilderness that incorporates upper Bonita Pines with the lowlands of the Hemville area.

The three experienced middle-aged hikers were walking the popular Needle Lane trail when approached by five odd looking black wolves, who carried a wider gait and smaller ears. The wolf's short, black coats also set them apart from a typical fluffy Bonita Pines wolf.

"We just stood there, shocked at what we were looking at," says Mike Horowitz, one of the hikers. "Next thing we knew, three of them paired up with each of us and lunged."

"They successfully broke the skin at our necks and torsos, while the remaining two just howled. It took all we had to fight them off enough to reach for our pepper spray, which held them off enough for us to run," another hiker said.

The three ran a quarter mile to the ranger's office, where they were soon met by paramedics who treated the three before transporting them to a nearby hospital.

"We've seen Superwolves around this area before," said Ranger Michael Lehey. "A typical Superwolf – which is also known as a 'Coywolf' – is a cross breed of coyote and wolf."

The hybrid-breed is much more dangerous than their original species, as they carry the strongest characteristics of both – bred to hunt and survive through any elements. They've been turning up in greater numbers this year in the built-up areas of Eastern North America.

"Now, the difference between a Coywolf and what we saw attack the hikers today, is that there's a third element has been added to this gene pool, in the form of the over-brimming stray Pit Bull population that has been infesting the outskirts of Hemville, by Oakglen Road," he said.

Oakglen Rd. borders Hemville from The Preserve. Considering the proximity, it's been inevitable these Pits would eventually venture into our forests and not just pack up with other breeds of feral canines, but breed with them as well.

The result? A new 'SuperPitWolf' who carries not just the survival skills of the other crossbreeds, but the aggressive nature bred into Pit Bulls by notorious Hemville dogfighters."

"As we have now learned, these guys are not afraid of humans, unlike the previous Superwolf breeds who kept to their customary food chain," concluded Lehey.

Bonita Pines Preserve will be closed until further notice.

"Jesus, what next?" thought Richard. He folded the paper, slapping it on the table like he was swatting a fly.

He would have to think of an alternative to pass the weekend. Reading only made him want to write again, especially after reading that fantastical stuff going on his own neighborhood.

His mind began to accelerate, Tilt-a-Whirling what seemed like every scene in history through his head. Every doomed possibility with every false start hero who tried to fix it. Every victim and every single apathetic mass of de-humanity with every opinion that would do nothing but create a cacophony in calamity's favor.

He stopped it clean like a dealer with his roulette wheel, though the ball of course kept rolling.

It landed on a guy agonizing in front of his computer again, getting up to pace every five minutes, going outside to smoke every ten, before returning to the screen for another twenty.

This circular behavior, he could not stop.

He sat gazing, drenched once again in the glow of digital semi-literate jargon he would love today and hate tomorrow. Engaged. Possessed. Choke-held by his work, he had no idea that the sun had already been down for eleven hours when he saw the clock say 4:12am.

While it was nearly the next day, Richard would not see the sunrise. The Hour of the Wolf had come, the time between night and dawn where one's deepest fears would come to roost. Where demons and their personifications would be rendered most powerful. And their dreamers, most vulnerable.

He shut the computer off – the only light on in the house – as he tried to get undressed for bed in the disorienting black, just wanting to get it over with.

Balancing on one leg to remove his jeans, Richard fell over, startled by Chipper going absolutely nuts, barking blue to warn his person.

"Shhhhhhh... Easy there, buddy."

It was always a transparent attempt to act like nothing was wrong, especially when Richard knew something was wrong.

He heard it outside, every corner of his house. A scattered violent scratching, A swelling chorus of howling. A feral, tuneless and painful barking.

Chipper had already done three spastic rounds of the perimeter. He was well onto his fourth when Richard got the balls to look out his bedroom window.

The house was now surrounded by a new kind of nature. A writhing, circling membrane of black canines – SuperPitWolfWhateverYouCall'Ems. Their sleek, dark coats, proud wolf manes. Their mouths peeled back to reveal protruding fangs, evolved to an even larger scale that began to make the wooden front door their fibrous appetizer. They had already tried and failed with the stucco around the sides, but this was like eating through cake.

Like demonic sperm fighting over the most vulnerable spot of an egg, they all collected at the door. They climbed atop one another, frantically gnawing at the splintering wood for the chance to be the first one to take a bite of fresh prey inside.

Richard scooped up Chipper and ran to the back patio. The hellhounds had a sixth sense, following him around the entire length of the chain link. Every time he stepped once, they stepped twice, always a step ahead; a staggered mirror image daring him to see the full reflection.

He collapsed in the middle of his living room, holding Chipper into his torso. He doubled over, in upright fetal position. He held onto his puppy so tight he thought he might hurt him, but he couldn't risk the susceptibility when they eventually entered.

Richard's last good deed that wouldn't go unpunished: being Chipper's human shield until there was nothing left of him in the house but a smeared crimson puddle.

**

As the sun rose that morning over Bonita Pines Preserve, postcard perfect shards of light shot through the trees, the rays suspended like scaffolding holding up the balance of nature. It gave warmth to an open meadow where twenty-two black Pit Wolves frolicked in an unruly yet relaxed cluster. Just finishing the last of their night's blood-seasoned bounty, the ones closest to the center watched with pride as their new member, a scrappy white Jack Russell, finally helped himself to some bones with plenty of meat on them still.

Chipper hesitated to chew, at first. For a while he would be content to lick the pungent essence of his person's marrow, his way of continuing to say thanks for rescuing him once again.

The Gutter Runs Internally

"After bouts of self-sabotage amidst their otherwise typical underground hell-raising, the long-awaited second LP from L.A. cow-punk swamp-glam leaders GUTTERSNAKE finally threatens to see the light of day. While other bands on Sunset Strip get by with shaking their ass, Guttersnake shakes their dice — blurring the lines between swashbuckling musicality, surrealistic lyricism and their notorious self-destructive lifestyle. With a new deal on Capitol Records, it could be the album that makes or breaks them. The big question: Can Guttersnake hold it together, or will it fray again like the decaying duct-tape on their shitkickers?"

Rock City News, April 1989

"Really? You booked us at Jimmy's place again?"

"You've gotta be kidding me! Were you that messed up the last time we played there? I was the one that had to deal with the guy..."

"Yeah, we got peanuts for a huge crowd, then we had to carry your drunk ass out of there..."

"Nope! Not doing it. You can bang on a floor tom while you sing or something..."

Johnny Rising had already been on his last DT nerve at rehearsal before he started getting the third degree from his bandmates just for relaying the show offer. Their band Guttersnake were asked to play Darwin's Dancehall by the owner/booker Jimmy Darwin, an L.A. impresario who was as infamous as he was nefarious. Darwin didn't just make a killing at his club – he had multiple hustles going in and out of the venue that had nothing to do with live music or alcohol sales, depending on who you asked.

Unless your live band is Guttersnake and you're fueled by Darwin's cocaine, heroin, and all the free drinks you can drink, as long as you can stand.

One would think with all that money coming into the club, especially from extra hard cash of slinging hard drugs, there would be an overabundance of cash flowing to pay the bands well, especially since they were the ones bringing the loose wallets into the venue. But Jimmy Darwin fueled his drug trade capital by exploiting bands first, often taking advantage of the more naive groups who would be seduced by the 'exposure' the Dancehall's built in crowd could offer, even if they might be seeing three of you by the time they came in.

Johnny actually knew Jimmy well. Not friends, just pure business. But the business was frequent, when Johnny would hand over a weekly wad of cash for the group's insidious speedball habit. He liked him as a dealer, but not as a promoter – a conflict of interest that blew up the last time they played the Dancehall.

As the most notorious cow-punk band in town, Guttersnake didn't just sell the place out that night – it was oversold. It looked like a big pay day for them by the end of the night, but after consulting the box office, the numbers just didn't add up. The four of them, minus Johnny, refused to leave the counting room until they got their guarantee plus backend. Johnny had walked out in frustration to keep drinking, helping himself to a bottle of whiskey off the wall behind the bar.

"I'll just fucking drink it out of you," he yelled as he leaned over the bar. At 2:45 am there were no bartenders there to stop him.

After a twenty-minute interrogation, bassist Charlie

Gone finally got Jimmy to admit that he often let people in for free – namely, his other customers; if they buy a bag, they can hang out as long as they want as long as they're buying drinks.

"So, let me get this straight," Charlie started. "We sell the place out, there's a line going all the way around the block of people who can't even get in, just because you got your other people in there taking up space who don't even know who were are, and we're still not getting our full but low-balling $500 guarantee when we should be getting about a fucking grand?"

"I know, I know... Listen, what if I bump it up to $450, and I'll give you a fat bag o' horse and blow – it'll be worth $600 with the cash included?" Jimmy was an expert at making it look like he was negotiating in your favor when he was robbing you blind, and he knew these guys were jonesing.

"I mean, you know just as well as I do that you were gonna give me that money right back for some dope anyway..." he reasoned. "I'm saving you a step, is all!"

The four of them uttered a silent simultaneous *fuck* because they knew he was not exactly *right,* but that he had them by the balls.

Before they could seal the imbalanced deal, an empty bottle of Jim Beam went flying into the box office, nearly missing Jimmy's head. Jimmy's arms went flying into the four of them, assuming it was one of the four until Johnny came in, cutting in with a stabbing ham-fisted windmill.

The racket echoed through the main stage room, reaching Jimmy's token Mexican bouncer who was taking a leak. He ran to the box office, breaking it up with piss on his hands. A large, imposing human brick wall, he was able to scoop them up like a tractor and get them all out while they pathetically continued hitting him – the contrast of force relegating them to the weakness of children. Charlie dragged Johnny out before he did more damage to Jimmy to keep them from getting paid. But out they went, into the alley, forfeiting their loot because they lost their cool as the door slammed shut behind them.

***

"Okay, listen... I know it was bad last time, but Jimmy wants a truce," Johnny said, continuing his gig pitch. "I think we can stand to make a lot of money this time because..."

"Dude, he only wants us to play because of our cover story in Rock City News this month! And the date of the show is the 30th?" Charlie pleaded. "You see how he's already trying to take advantage of us again? He's a total opportunist!"

"Okay, listen..." James, the lead guitarist chimed in. "I don't like the idea of this, but what if we did the show at the Dancehall on that Thursday, but also set up a secret show at the Warehouse downtown for that Saturday as insurance? You know we always make good money there."

"Yeah, I can see that," Billy the drummer concurred. "If Jimmy thinks it's okay to double-dip, then why can't we? We just gotta make sure that we don't announce the warehouse show until the day before so he don't pull any radius clause bullshit. We'll just call everyone in our black books."

"Okay, cool!" said Johnny. "We'll take advantage on Jimmy's promo machine to get the word out to the press for *his* show, but then *our* show that Saturday can be a more intimate affair with hopefully some spillover hype from the Dancehall."

"Okay, I guess?" said Charlie. "I don't feel great about this, but I guess we'll just do it all over again... Uh, and speaking of doing something all over again, who needs a fix? We're done rehearsing, right?"

The other four agreed, already salivating to get their nightly dose. They broke out their works, fired up, then shot up in a supportive ritual circle as they engaged in light scene gossip.

"So, Johnny, is that Lisa chick still stalking you?"

"Oh God, I hope not..." Johnny replied. "I haven't seen her in about a week, so I guess that's a good sign."

"Is that when she was digging through your trash? Man, next time she digs through your garbage, the cops should be notified immediately."

"Yeah, I know. I've been way too nice. Mark my words I'll call 'em next time. I just don't want heat at our house at all in case they wanna search the place for whatever reason."

"It's cool man, we know how sweet she was when you first met her. But she's a fan, not a friend. You definitely shouldn't have slept with her. I saw this coming from a mile away."

"Whatever, man, let's just get out of here before they make us pay for an extra hour," said Johnny as he helped Billy disassemble his drums.

As they opened the rehearsal space door, a waft of fog-drenched night cooled the sweat off the faces, refreshing their highs into a near-invincible feeling.

Until they tripped over her legs, causing a bumbling collision.

"Hi hi hi!!"

It was Lisa, sitting with her legs stretched out across the walkway, rapidly waving both hands like some cruel Al Jolson shit.

Buzzkill, they all thought. Johnny turned around, acting like he forgot something.

"Sounded great, guys! I could hear everything actually really good out here, just like wearing earplugs or something..."

"Lisa! You can't keep doing this!" Charlie scolded. "Johnny's not interested and you gotta stop following us around..."

"I heard you guys are gonna play Darwin's Dancehall on the 30th?" she said, changing the subject.

"What? You heard that all the way from out here? You had your ear to the door, great!"

"Yeah, Lisa... you gotta split. We'll see you at the show, but you're not invited to our rehearsals, please. Leave now, so Johnny can leave too. You freak him out, you know."

"Okay! See you at the show! Both shows!" she said, cheerfully walking backwards before she went on her way. She was incorrigible, her smile and enthusiasm her shield against reality.

"Coast clear, Johnny!" Charlie hollered.

***

Thursday the 30th arrived quickly. Johnny scheduled one more rehearsal for that morning. It was a deviation from their usual rule: practicing the day of show is bad juju, wasting their pent up psycho-sexual energy on the walls of the rehearsal space instead of a sold-out club. But Johnny had a surprise for them.

He told them all to close their eyes. They heard him scrambling, little sounds of metal and leather on the thin stained carpet.

"Okay, open 'em!"

In front of each instrument, lay their new one – a Ruger old-style Vaquero .45 with an elaborately embroidered holster that spelled out Guttersnake in turquoise and pearl.

"Holy shit! Are these real?"

"Real as we are," Johnny replied pridefully. "Not like these pansy-glam bands we get forced to play with. We are taking this cowboy punk thing to a whole other level!"

They hated the hair metal scene that continued to infiltrate *their* Sunset Strip. The Guttersnake guys did have big-ratted hair, but they dressed like leather and denim bandana-clad Road Warriors – like futuristic Caballeros, priding themselves on blurring the lines of the punk rocker lifestyle and old Western grit. These guns would make them untouchable kings of the L.A. rumor-mill, and once again, it would all be true.

"I mean, if these new gangster rappers are doing it, why can't we?" Johnny reasoned, as if he needed to inject any logic into his bandmates. They were already whipping around with their new toys, rehearsing the moves of their new advanced status, legends in their own minds now with tools to enforce it on other's reality if they had to.

But who were they kidding? As tough as the guns made them feel, they probably wouldn't go beyond shooting cans in the back alley after the show. The important part is that people would be *talking* about the fact that they ran strapped.

***

"Hell yeah," Johnny said, as he looked out the window of the Dancehall's green room upstairs. "There's already a line going all the way around the block and it's not even 7pm!"

"Where's Charlie?" asked James.

"Oh, he's taking his own numbers!" assured Johnny. "He's down there actually counting people as they walk in. He made sure all Jimmy's usual crowd paid tonight."

"Tight ship!" said Billy.

Johnny was in haughty-form leading up to the show – sporting his one-of-a-kind Guttersnake T-shirt he made in the early days. The graphic was an anatomical depiction of a ribcage – in perfect placement of his own – with a hissing serpent intertwined through the bone. His personal artistic commentary that the *gutter lives inside us all.*

Once 7pm hit, the green room began to fill with the Gutt's inner circle of bollo-tied dipso-desperados, raccoon-eyed death-rock chicks, and a couple nameless hangers-on that Billy let in to make things interesting. He volunteered to drink by the door to make sure that crazy Lisa chick wasn't one of them.

The green room quickly smeared into a chattering commune of toxic euphoria, like a race to see who could feel the most invincible in the shortest amount of time. Time, in fact, tends to cease to exist when you live this fast – which is why they were all shocked to get the frantic knock on the door.

"Oh shit guys, we're on!" hollered Billy, looking at his Swatch watch.

The five of them grabbed as many beers as they could hold. Billy swiped a communal bottle of Jack as their party crew followed behind them, like an entourage for a prize fight.

***

A familiar yet precarious scene – the box office at Darwin's Dancehall after hours. The five of them loaded up the van, impatiently awaiting the night's totals, not bereft of dread for their past treatments from Jimmy. But the sold-out show gave them enough high hope to consider letting their guard down.

Jimmy emerged from the office with an expression of profound defeat.

"Oh, don't fucking tell us!" Charlie said.

"Guys, I'm really sorry but I'm in a bit of trouble here..." he said, shaking his head, refusing to make eye contact.

"You've gotta be kidding me!" Johnny screamed. "There's no possible excuse!"

"You guys, listen... it was a great night. The best night I've had you..."

"Yeah, and now we're being *had* once again, right?" quipped Johnny.

"I'm just gonna come right out and ask," said Jimmy in earnest. "Can you guys do me a favor and give me, say, a week to pay you?"

"What? Why?"

"I'm in big trouble with my supplier. I owe them $2000 for the last batch they fronted me last month, and they're threatening me if I don't pay them by noon tomorrow. These are... really bad guys, you understand? I'm afraid this is a life and death thing for me."

"What? You're full of it, man!" Charlie said as he stepped closer. "Why should we be responsible for another night of you mismanaging your funds? And no, wait... a better question – why should we even believe you?"

"You guys," Jimmy began to tear up. "These guys have guns. They kill people."

"Well guess who else has guns?" Johnny said, grabbing his pistol out the holster. He stomped over to Jimmy, pressing the barrel into his temple.

CLICK!

"What, is that some kind of toy gun, you fucking clown?"

Before Charlie had a chance to restrain him, Johnny

pulled the trigger of his very much not a toy gun, giving the hole-ridden conscience of Jimmy Darwin the biggest – but finally – the most tangible hole of his life. A spray of brain and blood instantly covered the wall outside the box office as he collapsed to the floor.

"Oh my fucking God, Johnny!! What did you do?" As if the echo of the shot wasn't loud enough, Charlie's volume would further incriminate them in the incident.

"Hey! What the fuck is going on?" screamed the bouncer. They could hear him leaving the front door.

The second he saw the bouncer throw open the door to the main room, Charlie panicked, firing twice. One bullet hit the man's shoulder, throwing him off balance. The next one hit the top of his head in mid-fall to the floor. He twitched, then went still.

"Fuck! What are we doing?" Charlie said. He looked up to the ceiling, screaming to a God who would not answer.

Their three bandmates rushed in through the back door from the alley where they were shooting bottles. They had heard three shots that weren't theirs but saw the grizzly scene to realize it *was* theirs, solidarity-wise.

Now, they *were* a gang.

They ran around with their hands on their temples, like plugging their ears from an unescapable new reality.

Time stood still for Johnny, as he just stared at his Guttersnake shirt, now splattered heavily in the blood of the Jimmy Darwin. He didn't mean to kill the guy – he just wanted Jimmy to take him seriously, for once. But he thought back to the tears that had welled up in Jimmy's eyes, as he pled for help and understanding. An ulcerous pain grew in his stomach as he realized how sincere he looked for once. Johnny had never seen that kind of vulnerability in Jimmy – a weak spot his shadow side saw to finally get even with him.

He heard them screaming his name, breaking him

from his introspection.

He thought quick.

"Okay, don't touch a damn thing!" he said. "Charlie, start the van. Everyone jump in the van and I'll be right there!"

Johnny ran toward the box office, jump-stepping over Jimmy's body as he went inside. He grabbed the overflowing till, scooping out the cash into the stacks in mid-count on the desk.

He shoved it all into every pocket on his leather jacket, then his jeans, but ran out of room quickly until he shoveled the rest down his pants, which were tight enough to hold it all. Johnny had experienced every kind of hedonistic state one could think of, but he now knew the arousal of his well-hung cock being swaddled in tight wads of cold hard greenback.

He ran to the front door. He took the bottom right of his T-shirt – the only part that was not covered in blood – to wipe down the door in case they left fingerprints. He kicked it open with his boot and ran out as the door swung shut behind him. He jumped in the van and removed his bloody shirt.

"Okay, listen... the quicker we all get to our own apartments, the better alibis we'll have." Johnny explained. "The one saving grace we've got is that Jimmy was already running from some bad motherfuckers, so if you think about it, I just made it look like a robbery – like those guys were collecting their debt."

"Jesus, I mean... shouldn't we skip town until this all blows over?"

"No, no way!" said Johnny. "It'll look bad if we disappear. That would be an admittance of guilt. We gotta just hold tight tomorrow and go ahead and do the gig downtown on Saturday. You guys with me?"

They all put their hands in the middle of their formation. They clasped them so hard it was difficult to let go.

Charlie dropped off Johnny first. He jumped out, eyes growing moist as he saluted them.

James rolled down the window. He threw his shirt at him. "Man, get rid of this damn thing, will you?"

Johnny caught the shirt. He ran to the side of his apartment and threw it in the garbage can. He would deal with it in the morning, but for now his mind was racing as to what might seem incriminating, out of character or off-kilter should this all come crashing down. Or was he overthinking it all? Would it be the strangest thing if he emptied the trash into the dumpster in back? He was already opening his door. He would have a shot first, to let this all sink in as gently as possible.

***

He awoke to the cruelest morning. A dawn of uncertainty, but what was assured was that it was not just a bad dream.

He saw the clock – almost noon. He had forgotten to throw the trash in the dumpster.

He bee-lined down his stairs, grabbing the can like a hot potato and threw it in the green dumpster in back.

Real *natural*-like.

He ran back up, skipping stairs. When he returned, he flipped on the news as he poured some Fruit Loops. Nothing reported on last night's accident, but it was only a matter of time. He couldn't stand it. He went into his room and busted out his works, when a new kind of dread befell him.

There was only enough for one more shot.

He exhaled heavily. Not only did he kill the most

notorious club owner in town, but it just now dawned on him he had severed the main channel of dope into his veins.

He was gonna get sick on top of all of this. He called the guys. Their shooting cycles were so well-synched that they were all in the same dire scenario. His panic for supply quickly distracted him from the panic that they had murdered two men, but eventually it all swirled into a new kind of toxic darkness that locked him to his couch after shooting the last bit.

***

Saturday came.

Crawling.

In the last thirty hours, none of the five could recall if they slept for more than an hour at a time. They were too paranoid to keep their guns, yet too panicked to get rid of them. They continued their costumed charade as Charlie made the rounds to pick everyone up for the show. He picked up Johnny first.

"You good, man?"

"I'd be better if I could score..."

"Yeah, well I tried everything and the best I could score us was a little speed, but it'll get all of us off and get us through this show, at least. We'll be tweaking too hard to withdraw, you know?"

"Uh, no... I *don't* know."

"Well, it'll just be fucking different, okay?"

They picked up James – usually the quiet one. But they saw him mumbling something under his breath as he walked up to the van. He stepped in, erupting with profanity as he pointed his gun to Johnny's temple.

"Well, guess who I'm gonna fucking shoot when I start kicking tonight? You fucking blew it, man! For all of us!"

Charlie stopped the van as the three of them restrained him, pressing him into his seat as he breathed heavy through his clenched teeth, eyes still locked on Johnny's downcast face.

When they arrived at the Warehouse they hid out in the van for as long as they could.

Ten minutes before their set, they gathered in the bathroom of the warehouse, haggard and jagged. Charlie cut up five lines. They vacuumed it up like vets, each one asking other, "You good?" about a hundred times. They all hooted and hollered, the cavalier transparent. Billy drummed on each of their backs with his hands as they walked on the stage.

They picked up their instruments as the crowd stepped closer into the radiance of the stage lights. That's when Johnny saw her.

It was Lisa, wearing his one-of-a-kind Jimmy Darwin Signature Blood Splattered Guttersnake T-Shirt, beaming wildly like she had found the Holy Grail of Groupie Gold.

Johnny jumped off the ledge, landing on Lisa as he began tearing the shirt off her body, peeling the moth-eaten gauzy strips, her throes of ecstasy, of received attention, unable to register on the crowd who closed in, intervening with this perceived sexual assault – despite it being worse than that, despite it being accessory to murder, despite her loving every aggressive rip of his stolen fabric rubbing against her skin, his flesh now touching hers. He hadn't given her this much attention since that one night, so she started kissing him hard to claim him, hoping to level out the fists from the crowd pummeling his head, this megalomaniac singer whose last screw went loose – they thought *he* thought every girl was up for grabs, so they pulled her away, she started screaming NO but no one knew she was saying NO cause she didn't want him to stop they just heard NO so they carried her to safety outside while the crowd took turns beating him senseless. The rest of the Gutts finally broke from their tweaked-out paralysis and jumped in, only to make it worse – it just made more options for more fists, to beat the shit out of the most popular glam-punk band in Los Angeles who finally crossed the line, whose only sophomore recording would be an interrogation room confession.

Wino's Shadow

No one really wants to know anybody in Los Angeles, not who they really are beneath their masks. That's why the anti-social types go to Happy Hour, to escape, not be bothered. It's a quirk native to that city – even with drink specials, an L.A. bar can't attract a crowd at 5pm... No one wants to be caught dead early to the nightlife – if you're not fashionably late to anything, it looks like you had nothing better to do. Like you maybe didn't put on enough make-up.

She gave herself one last look in a rear-view of a new Toyota Camry parked and ticketed in the alley of The Powerhouse bar. "Ugh, honey – you got so sweaty out there," she whispered, applying more foundation that kept turning to angel food batter on her cheeks.

Inside, Carter Campbell sat at the bar, on his second Greyhound at 5:16. He swiveled his head around, surveying the room through its dim lighting, trying to zero in on the usual suspects – the real alcoholics who needed the two-hour window just to deal with the gravity of nightfall.

"Where's, uh… that one thing tonight?" he asked the bartender.

"Excuse me?"

"You know, that… I don't know whether it's a guy or a girl…"

"Listen, if you're talking about Amy, have some fucking class and don't call her an *it,* okay? If someone has the skill to wear a mini-skirt and heels as well as Amy does, well I'd call that a woman. End of story."

Carter put his palms up in surrender. "Man, I apologize. I didn't mean any disrespect. It's just hard to get used to…"

"There's nothing to *get used to*" said the bartender. He mimicked Carter's palms up, shaking them into insulting jazz-hands. "At the end of the day, Amy's more welcomed here than you are. Hell, she practically lives here."

Barely a beat and the doors swung open.

"I TOLD YOU… I WAS TROUBLE!!!" Amy's arms hung in crucified pageantry at the entrance. Eyes: wing tipped. Black beehive, red lipstick on a triumphant grin reveling in the sparse applause from the three other regulars. The bartender clapped the loudest.

"Amy! Go good out there I take it?"

"Honey, you know I'm no good," she said, striding to the bar. "But yeah, you can say I *did* good!" Her hands scrambled then emerged from her purse, fanning out a peacock tail of cash.

"All right, baby," said the bartender. "Here's your victory cola, on the house!"

"Now just 'cause I had a good day, don't go sneaking booze in there, you know I don't like that shit anymore!"

"Never. Not until the day you tell me to again, Amy."

Carter smirked. He was starting to get it – he even had a copy of *Back to Black* out in his car, one of his favorite albums. He caught Amy's eye, motioning her to waddle over.

"Hey, I've seen you so many times and it's just now dawning on me – you're trying to be Amy Winehouse, right?"

Amy scoffed. "Ugh, *trying?* Honey, just because you have a profound spiritual and karmic connection with someone doesn't mean you're *trying* to be like them!"

"Oh, shit… sorry. Didn't mean to offend."

"Well, you bloody did!"

"Oh, you got the British accent and everything? Nice. So, you're like, trans?"

"Transcontinental, maybe!" she said. "But my

personality's so large it jumps the fucking ocean, so *of course* I'm gonna have a bit of a British accent."

"So, wait… where are you from originally?"

"I'm from Amy, baby. You can say she gave birth to me."

"Okay, fine – but what state?"

"State…" she rolled her eyes. "Amy *is* a state. A state of mind. A state of fashion. State of the art. A state of just… being!"

Carter realized he was out of his element, his curiosity making a fool of himself. He focused his attention on finishing his drink instead. Amy stirred her Coke, took a bit of the maraschino, then swallowed the whole thing – quickly realizing she was starved for attention, not candied fruit.

"Okay fine, nosy! I was born in Kansas City."

Carter was distracted, ordering another Greyhound.

'I *said* I was born in Kansas City!"

"Oh, sorry…" he said, facing her again. "That's cool, what side?"

"Well, for a while there it was the sui-cide…"

He got nervous. "Well, whatever side, it's a great border city."

'Oh yeah, all the doctors call me Borderline, that must be why. Always on the edge, baby!"

Carter smirked. *Amy is hilarious*, he thought – *but also, totally fucking serious, isn't she?*

"Right on. So, what brought you to L.A., Amy?"

"You know, just to be myself, really." Her accent had gone full slobbering cockney. She launched into press interview mode. "Once I really started coming into my own in KC, I had a harder time being who I really am. See, I prefer to be the loudest one in the room. I started running out of places that would let me. I was kicked out of every bar in town. I was putting *all* the sass in Kan-sass, it was a lot of work. But they didn't know real talent when they see it, so I left. They didn't deserve me anyway.

"Got it. But why do you even hang out in bars – looks like you don't drink?" he said, pointing to her Roy Rodgers.

"Oh, that's just for now. It's only because Amy is in trouble – she's trying to get sober for real this time, you know? I don't want to be a bad influence on her."

"You mean, the real Amy Winehouse, right?"

Amy looked up, then down. "I mean *both* of us. When I say 'Amy,' I speak for two. Two black hearts that beat as one."

Carter was really getting it now, coming to acceptance. He didn't quite know what to say next, but Amy took care of the silence.

"See, The Powerhouse here is like my office. You'll usually see me here every other hour to take a break, unless I'm really moved by the spirit out there."

"Out where?"

"Oh, our little runway – right in front of Mann's Chinese, sometimes in front of Hollywood and Highland."

Another constellation formed in Carter's nodding head. He knew that pseudo-iconic scene where the impersonators preyed on gawking tourists, hustling them for a paid photo op. There was the arrogant glassy-eyed Superman, the Batman with anger-management issues, a couple of rivaling Marilyn Monroes who split the am/pm shifts to stay out of each other's wigs, then the near-perfect Captain Jack Sparrow, who was ravenously popular since *Pirates of the Caribbean: On Stranger Tides* had just come out that May.

"Aha, got it," he said, throwing back a hearty gulp of the Greyhound. "That's some stiff competition over there.

How does Winehouse compete with Jack fucking Sparrow?"

"Oh, we don't! I hang to myself and just sing my little heart out – not like those fools in Under-roos have any real talent, so I kinda stand out. The crowd I get might be a little smaller but it's much hipper. And since I'm still alive – a real live pop star – you know a lot of them are taking those photos and telling people they really met me."

"Ha! Right. If you're putting one over on people, why shouldn't they?" Carter began raising his glass to Amy's; she appeared to be obliging his toast until she kept raising it to his face.

"Honey, the only thing I'm gonna put over anyone is this drink over your head if you don't stop disrespecting me."

"Woah, hold on… stop. Listen, I'm sorry. Really." He changed his approach – he wasn't playing the game as well as he thought. "I haven't even had the chance to tell you what a big fan I am of yours."

Amy blushed, on queue. "Oh, is that right? What's your favorite song?"

"Well… let's just say I've actually been to *Rehab* and I've gone *Back to Black*, so those two songs cut particularly deep for me."

"Aw, you good now though, right?" she said, her first signs of genuine care told him he had broken a wall down with his opening up.

"Yeah, I think so. Booze helps. Until it doesn't."

"Ain't that the truth. No matter what you love, you love it too much – it's a losing game."

He wouldn't dare call her an act at this point, but Carter was impressed with her lines, the way she was flipping Winehouse song titles into little bits of nihilist philosophy. *Is it even an act when you're always 'on'?* he wondered.

"So where do you live, Amy?"

She opened her mouth. Nothing came out.

"Like, you know… what part of town?"

She whipped her head to the side, bangs veiling her eyes.

"I live… in me?" she said, cocking one eye through her jet-black hair. "I live in Amy. Wino's my religion, therefore my body and clothes are my temple. My church. My shelter."

Carter ordered another drink, downed it in two gulps. Even with the lush cushion of vodka drowning his mind, he was disarmed – Amy was sort of breaking his heart. He noticed it was sprinkling outside, against the windows. Saved by the rain.

"Well, speaking of shelter, I should get going home before that rain gets too crazy," he said, tonguing the last drips from his ice.

"I feel you. I'll walk you out," she said.

Carter paid his tab, offering to pay for Amy's. The bartender smiled, one hand gesturing, *"Nah, that's sweet but we got her."*

The two emerged into the alley into a mounting downpour. "Damn!" said Carter. "Guess June Gloom turned into June Hysterics, huh?"

"Sure, but my name ain't June, baby," said Amy, winking. "You know that by now. By the way, what's your name?"

"Oh, it's Carter. Carter Campbell."

"All right Carter Campbell. I'm gonna call you CC."

"Ha, that's cool with me, A-Dub." Carter's smile quickly grimaced. "Ah man, what the fuck!" He grabbed the ticket off his windshield wiper.

"Oh no! I saw that on my way in, didn't realize it was your car…"

"I *just* fucking bought this thing too…"

She noticed the *Back to Black* CD on his passenger

seat. "Oh yeah, 2011? Well, you might just get some pennies from heaven, then. Just like the rain, tears gonna dry on their own."

"Huh?"

"How much is the ticket, CC?"

He unfolded the flimsy paper. "Fucking sixty bucks!"

She reached into her purse, flipped through her flush stack. She extended three crisp twenties into his hand."

"What is this? Nah, I can't let you do this, Amy."

"You didn't let me do anything, CC. It's already done," she said, winking with a smirk. She turned around, shielding her towering Bump-it from the rain with her purse, began walking off.

"Hey! Can I at least give you a ride somewhere?"

Her one hand gestured, *"Nah that's sweet but I got me…"*

Carter leaned against his bumper. He stared at the three twenties, dumbfounded by the kindness, yet unsettled by it. He had a good-paying job downtown, yet an eccentric homeless person just turned him into a charity case. He didn't feel above it – he felt unworthy.

He thought quick: *If she's going back to work the tourists in the rain like this, I'll somehow disguise myself and just give it back to her.*

He stuck the ticket back on his windshield. He ran to the corner, saw she was just crossing Highland. He sprinted to the corner store – one of those cheap tourist shops – grabbed a blue Dodgers umbrella, handed the clerk one of the twenties, grabbed the three fives back. He walked back outside, looked to the right – he could still see her pink outfit darting through the foot traffic, crowds scrambling to escape the rain.

Carter frantically unbuttoned the umbrella as he ran to catch up with her. It bloomed open like a Morning Glory as he crossed Highland, right in time – he noticed Amy stopping a block ahead in front of the mall. She grabbed a glass jar from a planter, then posted up against the marble to get in her groove.

Carter leaned his umbrella forward to conceal her potential view. But her voice made its way to his ears – the opening line of "Tears Dry on Their Own," the perfect tune to garner sympathy in the rare L.A. downpour. *"All I can ever be to you/is the darkness we once knew/and this deep regret I had to get accustomed to."*

What her voice lacked in tonal accuracy, she made up for it in volume. Slightly more baritone but in the pocket. In fact, Amy had more control and anchor to her voice than the real thing, a brassy sweep of devoted emotion not about to be drowned out by the monsoon hitting the pavement, nor the booming thunder above. By the time she kicked the chorus in, Amy had drawn a crowd of five people as Carter walked into shrouded view.

He lifted his umbrella to get a view of her tip jar, took a few steps forward, put the $55 back to its source. He was just stepping back to give her voice the space it deserved, when another voice behind him cat-called Amy, mocking her performance. It was a young couple, day-drunk, heckling Amy through an amoral meat-grinder.

She stopped. "Excuse me?"

The hip couple laughed. "Sorry, but you're actually too good! It's not really accurate."

"What is that supposed to mean?" she said, hand on hip.

"Oh… you didn't see Winehouse's performance last night, the one from Belgrade?"

"Uh, nooo… I was busy!"

"Well, she fucking blew it!" the guy said. "She's either back on the sauce or back on dope or both, but she was out there just… out of it. Couldn't sing, or even remember her own words…"

"He's trying to say that she was fucking retarded!" said the girl, her guy covering her mouth. The couple began a shameful struggle until the girl wiggled out of his grasp.

"No! I want to show this bitch how she was acting on stage so she can learn!"

The girl stomped up to Amy, bellowing cruel moans into her face as tears welled up, her red lips wincing, her persona crumbling. Carter panicked behind his own blue wall of coverage. What he meant to be a chivalrous act had become one of cowardice – he bailed, conflicted, convincing himself the anonymous payback was more vital than defending her dignity. The more the rain beat down, the harder he scolded himself, all the way back to his car.

***

On July 23rd, Carter found himself in his usual seat at the bar of the Powerhouse, doing what he'd been doing every week – consoling Amy for her recent bad streak that began a month prior with that *fucking drunk white bitch*. "I should have just fucking hit her, but instead I hit the bottle," she said, lifting her rum and Coke. "Now look, still fuckin' hittin' it…"

"Here, hit this," said Carter, clinking his glass to hers. "Listen, give yourself a break. Nothing wrong with having a damned drink. Just quit demonizing the stuff – that's when it gets its real power over you. When was the last time you've even paid for one, anyway? People love you, Amy. We love you. You just gotta live where the love is."

She flashed him a ghost of a smile. "Aw, thanks CC. You know I appreciate that. It's not even that I feel like I'm slippin', more like I'm sliding away…"

"Pfft, I'll say. Now you're quoting that Paul Simon dork instead of our beloved Winehouse? Careful!" he said, a joking glare that finally got her to laugh, though she couldn't maintain eye contact.

"Hey Amy, can I ask why you keep looking over to that table in the corner?"

She did that thing – opened her mouth but no words came out. She shook her head, loosening her lines.

"Oh, you mean at Jim and Cisco right there?"

"Uh, I guess? I didn't know you knew 'em. Seems like every time they're here they're giving you stink eye."

"Oh, they're just sore I don't talk to them anymore. Long story, don't worry about it."

"Here, watch my drink, I'm gonna take a leak," he said, tapping his tumbler.

Amy nodded, finally making eye-contact as he got up, whipping her head right back to Jim and Cisco. Once she got their attention, she held up a twenty like ringing a bell. They smiled, motioning her over.

Carter entered the one-stall restroom that reeked of vomit and wet tobacco, only accentuated by the mentholated urinal cake he was pissing on. He had switched to beer since he was in for a long night at the bar, making his stream longer than usual. He checked his phone, right to Twitter, his compulsive habit even when he had a spare couple seconds. That's all the time it took to see it.

Amy Winehouse, dead at 27.

He nearly dropped his phone, his private world colliding with international headlines. The thought of Amy – both of them – scared him into paralysis as he held his cock, which was quickly turning into the world's tiniest violin, as they say. He snapped out of it, put it away, zipped up his pants, walking through a thick psychic gravity as he made his way back to the bar where he'd have to tell Amy the bad news.

It was already on the TV. She was already crying. The bartender was already giving her another rum and Coke, turning the volume up with the other. Jim and Cisco's yellowed teeth, already clenched.

There was nothing to say that a silent embrace couldn't say better. Carter walked up to Amy, put his arms around her, his chin in her nape. It only made her bawl harder. Devastated, then embarrassed she was being such an open wound, she removed her face from her palms.

"Keep 'em coming! Two more!" she said, her voice quivering strangely, a reveal of buried baritone. It was the first time Carter or the bartender heard her drop the accent.

"Whatever you need, Amy. Just let us know…" Carter and the bartender's sentiments overlapped into blurry inflections, submitting to the malaise.

"I need this to not be my fault! Why do I feel like this is all my fault?" she said, throwing back the stiff drink, her Adam's apple undulating over the flood.

"Wait, why would you say this is your fault?"

"You wouldn't understand," she said. Despite her slurring, Carter knew it was the truth.

"Amy, you wanna get up front there and do a song?" asked the bartender.

"I thought I wasn't allowed anymore!"

"I'm the boss here and I say you can, just for tonight. Let it out."

"Hell yeah, Amy. This is your moment. Do it for Amy," said Carter. He was rubbing her back for both encouragement and concern, the way she kept slurring. "What's that? What are you trying to say?"

"I said, '*everything I fucking do is for Amy*,' idiot! Fine, I'm going up!"

She threw her purse on the bar, wiggled off her stool.

She stumbled once, nearly turning her ankle in her high heel. The Powerhouse had gotten crowded since Carter's bathroom break, heads turned as she made her way through the crowd, up to the front by Jim and Cisco's table. She hesitated, knowing they'd be front row for this. "Fuck it!", she said, forgetting her thoughts had escaped the confines of her head.

She opened her mouth, but nothing came out – a sudden deer in headlights seeing how many people there were, transfixed on her, on what was about to happen. She'd never had this much immediate attention in front of Mann's Chinese. And right now, there was no more competition – she was the only Amy.

She began to belt, a combination of two songs, stumbling over the lyrics, forgetting which one she meant to do. Then she stopped, confused what she was doing up there.

"You got this, Amy! We got you!" hollered Carter.

But she didn't have it. She'd merely had herself. Her, in her sexy nurse Halloween outfit she bought at Hollywood Toy and Costume that she dyed pink, written *Amy* in Sharpie above the breast pocket, her Bump-It unraveling behind like a comet trail lost its luster.

She tried again, but all that came out were determined moans before the only decipherable line: "I died a hundred times!"

Then a burp.

"What the fuck is this!" someone yelled. "This is in such bad taste, the poor woman just fucking died! Have some respect!"

"Yeah, real class act, bitch!" someone else said, twisting the knife.

"It ain't an act!" said Cisco, raising an eyebrow. He signaled Jim to the door, that they should be leaving, like *now*.

Amy deflated in tears, too weak to defend herself, much less stand. So, she tried walking, but she moved too fast and fell to a kneel.

"Ha! At least she brought someone to her knees in here!" someone yelled.

"Hey! Fuck off you piece of shit!" said Carter, running to peel her off the floor. She put her arms around him, a fleeting sense of safety. She smirked as he puppeteered her back to her feet, leading her back to the bar where she put her head down, resting on her arms.

"You all right'"" he whispered into her ear.

She nodded her head, slowly, wishing she could tell him thank you, that no one had ever stuck up for her like that, that he was her best friend, that she wished he would just kiss her, if not tonight, then maybe one night, but for now, she was just so tired, so no words would come out of her mouth.

"Just… let her sleep it off," the bartender said, scrunching his nose.

Carter's one hand remained on her back for comfort, the other with the bartender's remote. He toggled between the news channels, seeing who had the latest developments, who was best at picking at her bones, when he realized a half-hour had passed. He leaned his head down into Amy's, whispering her name.

Again.

And again.

Eyebrows slanted, he quickly put his ear to her mouth.

"Hey! She's not breathing!"

The bartender got on the phone, hit one-button for 9-11. "The fuck? She only had like, five drinks!" His eyes darted the room for Jim and Cisco, those vulture motherfuckers.

Without hesitation, Carter pulled her to the floor, put his mouth to hers to begin CPR. For a second, her consciousness stirred, just long enough to know she was finally getting what he always wanted, long enough to make one last wish, that in another life, there could have been another way.

Bottom's Up

In pursuit of excitement, not all nights out on the town are going hit that fever pitch you're looking for. In fact, some end just like they begin, depending on your company. Some people just live on a loop until the circle finally cracks for them.

"Bottom's up!" said Colton Myers, signaling the rest to down their shots. The six of them threw their heads back with whiplash gusto, emptying the grain-alcohol contents with substantial flair. Only Colton kept leaning back almost ninety degrees, as if he had to prove he was getting every last possible fume, causing an unsightly jutting from their huddle.

"Dude, what are you doing?" said Tony, who would be turning twenty-five at midnight. "You're like, doing The Limbo!"

"How looooooow can I go?" said Colton, doubling down into his lean. It was impressive if this was a yoga class, but this was a dive-bar and Colton always had to take everything further than it should. It was fucking embarrassing.

"Shit, catch him! He's gonna fall!"

The five of them lunged toward him like catching a toddler just learning to walk. But Colton faked them out, throwing his left leg back to catch himself, just like he always did.

"Ha! Gotcha!" he said. Colton pointed at all of them, scanning his finger slowly like a sniper. "Who wants another shot? I'm buying!"

Instead of waiting for an answer, he sway-walked over to the bar like wheat in the breeze. He ordered six more, this time tequila. Colton assumed they had all followed behind him until the bartender handed the shots over. Realizing he was up there alone, he signaled to their table with a *what the fuck* hand gesture.

"Man, we're all just now taking first sips of our fresh beers!" hollered Tony, shaking his head. He leans over to Eli, the newest guy in their circle. "Watch, he's going to take all those shots himself because we won't come over there."

Like clockwork, Colton flips them all a double bird, then downs all six shots, adding the pageantry of his ninety-degree lean for the last one.

"See, you guys get two middle fingers 'cause those were all doubles! Fuck you, I'm out!"

Colton didn't give a shit they were only on their fifth round of drinks – the night was young. Although Tony wasn't officially twenty-five yet, he and his friends were already acting like Senior Citizens.

It was fucking embarrassing.

He exited the Night Owl, impressed that he was maintaining the symmetric balance of both middle fingers over his shoulders as he passed through the threshold.

His shoulder clipped the door guy. "Oh, and fuck you too!" Colton slurred, convinced that the bouncer pushed him. "Look, I'm 86ing myself 'cause you don't even know how to do your job in time!" The guy could only giggle at Colton's incriminating reverse psychology. After watching him try fitting his keys in his car for ten minutes, his giggles graduated to full-belly laughs, signaling to others to gawk.

Finally, Colton felt the relief of its satisfying insertion, yet was confused why there was a crowd cheering for him outside the bar. He got self-conscious that it was all in jest, until a voice inside him interrupted.

They are cheering because you *are Colton and this is* your *night.*

With that, he shoved the key into the ignition.

First fucking try.

He turned the key. He revved the engine. They were still watching him, clapping and cheering raucously, just like his real friends should have been doing inside.

He hit the gas.

The crowd went wild.

He swerved momentarily, then corrected like a pro, surging his diluted adrenaline. He barreled down that dark country road where he knew it was a straight shot to the Get Down Lounge.

The lights faded behind him as he was swallowed into the black of night. The moon now far behind his acceleration, no horizon to separate the road from the night sky. The only thing to pop out of the formless black was the rhythm of broken lines in the road to his left – *blip, blip, blip* they went, to the syncopated-synth beat of *"I Ran (So Far Away)"* playing on the local oldies station.

But even the pulsing flash of the lines in the road eventually faded, replaced by the once towering telephone wires on either side of his wheels.

Ascension.

Now he truly belonged to the night sky. He planned to turn up the night, but it turned out the night was turning him up, his frequency of existence morphing into a new vibration. Though his intoxicated state was finally hitting him, it remained in the euphoria stage, paralyzing him from reacting to this apparent divine escalation.

The lights of the town and cities below him blurred, then reformed, graduating into stars that surrounded his windows. He had never seen anything so beautiful. He sat in auto-pilot, awe-struck as he surrendered to the experience of space – the emptiness, yet a vast completion of existence.

Soon, a distant line of light came into view. His new horizon rushing in, flipping the darkness of space like suspended lightning.

"Aurora Borealis comes in view..." sang the song. Though sometimes we get lyrics wrong, other times the lyrics get us wrong; as an eternal day of endless fire took up the view of his windshield. He looked to his left, then his right, making sure it was also appearing in his rear-view mirror. An infernal periphery, enveloping him like a boiling ocean. He and his car had made contact with this boundary of limitless, licking flame, though there was no collision up here – only a fusing followed by the elemental burn back into ash, filled with echoing screams of those sent here before him.

The collision happened back at the Night Owl – first with flesh, then another moving vehicle. Tony and the other four lay lifeless in the street, tire-trampled by Colton's vehicle. While his soul was given the privileged knowledge that Hell is actually entered from the sky, the only way he could prove it was with his two, stiff middle fingers lying limp over his driver's side window.

The Space Between Two and Three

As her vision rebooted with darkness, the expanse deceived its very presence. Then, varying depths of glitterlight she could only assume were stars. They grew in size, from pinpricks to nickels, until she realized they weren't growing – they were speeding towards her.

She had no arms to flinch with once the first layer passed her by.

Skye Connelly was now disembodied in the absolute surrender of pure consciousness. Once the residue of her Earthbound recall compared it to driving through a blizzard, that's when she knew that it was *her* that was speeding towards *them*.

But this too, did pass; like a nagging magnet pulling her into another indeterminate section of the vastblack. She gained rearview perspective without the swivel of a neck, humbled that even a million balls of burning gas could abandon her – though her ability to emote also began to dissipate. Unencumbered by any further weight of ups and downs; still, Skye Connelly ascended into a space beyond the stars, into an area of man-made illumination.

Rather, a celestial whirlpool of synthetic debris. Because satellites are geostationary, it is assumed that the signals they send from Earth travel there in a tidy orderly stream, then bounce back to the planet in similar discipline. But consider the Web – now the accumulated scaffolding of civilization – its velocity, concentration, and frequency of usage. No one on Earth can imagine the backsplash, the stray droplets of static information going rogue down an erratic stream and into the void. Invisible to mortal optics, this polluted ethereal river of slighted intelligence could only be confirmed by those caught in its undertow – the spirits of the departed. Ascending back into the stardust from which they came, every one of the deceased now heads right for this intersection of absolute detour, flung into a stillborn swirl of ever-suspended Big Bang.

A Purgatory of Techno-Refuse.

Skye's essence arrived there like a lost child on the first day of school, suddenly robbed of spiritual instinct. Her only option: improvisation, once she saw all the other stray clouds of gas were not much different than her. So playfully she mingled, overlapping with the veteran elements.

Until she saw actual little pieces of her Earth-self floating in the fray, like shards of a broken mirror.

She repelled herself from the gaseous masses once she realized that they too, were all trying to put themselves back together again.

***

It was two weeks after the funeral.

If you didn't count the largest detail, that Jaxon Baker's best friend Skye was no longer tethered to the Earth, it looked like nothing had changed.

Because two weeks later, Jaxon was still staring at her photos on her LIFECAST Observer – her social media account that had since become her unsettling digital tombstone, a still-life chronological montage where she now had zero control over the content.

Much less, the comments.

He typed another one as tears welled up in his eyes:
You were the most original person I've ever met, Skye. For someone who

seemed like they fell out of the sky above, it's somehow the most difficult thing in the world to accept that you eventually had to go back there.

He deleted it right away. Not because he didn't mean every word, but because he felt foolish after scrolling up and seeing everyone else – mostly those who barely knew her – riffing on her unique name. They all made sentimental puns that might make his look one dimensional. Or worse – suggest that he didn't have anything more profound to say. Another subconscious contest to prove who knew the dead girl better in this performative electro-wake with no end in sight.

But he *did* know her the best. He didn't have to prove it by writing juvenile graffiti on her wall. He had all his memories of Skye up there in his Brain: the oldest, most reliable, and thankfully, most private computer God ever created. He slammed his laptop shut in frustration, a vain gesture of finality. Yet he felt stuck between a hyphenated footnote of mourning, as if he was experiencing a fine print too small and detailed for inclusion in the Five Stages of Grief.

Jaxon, Skye and Marco were inseparable.

Now, there was only two.

Marco found himself in the overwhelming role of consoling Jaxon since he had an emotional head-start. In spite of her privacy, Marco had long confronted Skye about her reckless experimentation with UPLYFT – the popular yet controversial over-the-counter anti-depressant – so his grieving began when he gave up talking sense into her.

"So, like, what Stage of Grief do you think you're in then?" said Marco.

"I dunno, like, somewhere between four and five – in the middle of Depression and Acceptance, I guess?" said Jaxon, ashamed of his stagnation.

"Well, you probably feel stuck because you *are* stuck.

Let me ask you – how often are you creeping on her LIFECAST Observer? 'cause you know that's just gonna make it worse…"

"Man, honestly – if I'm not at work or talking to you, I am *on* that shit. I can't stop. I'm always worried about what you told me…"

"What? What did I tell you?"

"About a person's three deaths."

"Yeah? So, what about it?"

"Well, I can accept her first death – her body no longer working. I can see how all this is temporary at best," he said, motioning to his chest and torso with his two fingers. "I can even accept her second death – I might have had tears in my eyes that day, but I forced myself to watch every inch as they lowered her casket down into the ground. But a person's third death, the whole forgetting about them thing – that one I refuse to deal with. Can you blame me?"

"No, I understand," said Marco. "But you got it a little twisted. A person's third death isn't just us forgetting about them while we're alive. I don't really think that's possible the way we loved Skye. The third death would be you or I dying. Eventually all of Skye's loved ones will pass away, so we'll be unable to think about her anymore. That's the third death – her circle fading to we can no longer keep her inside."

Jaxon thought it over.

"I don't know, man. I've been taking UPLYFT and just like everyone's been complaining – my recommended doses barely work anymore. Maybe I should take as much as she did? At least I wouldn't miss her this bad…"

"Man, you sound ridiculous. You wanna die like all these fools? I really can't believe this UPLYFT stuff is still legal – a person can only get so happy, you know? It's no different from any other dope, man. You get so high that there's nowhere else to go except go die."

"I didn't mean to imply I'd actually kill myself, man. I mean, Skye was crazy enough to cook it up and shoot it. I don't have the guts to mess with needles anyway. I was just thinking I could take a bigger dose than usual, maybe it would just clear this fog so I could focus, gain some perspective."

"Okay, so you're saying you want to turn your brain *on* instead of off, right?"

"Yeah. Like, what if I made a ritual out of it with a slightly larger dose... might help me feel closer to her. See what happens, you know?"

While it was only a brief smirk, one that Jaxon tried to hide by pursing his lips, Marco saw he had gotten through to him. He threw his arm around him, patting him on the back.

"Damn, so does this mean I can finally have a night off or do I have to report back the second you can't handle your drugs?" said Marco, laughing.

***

Armed with a forty of malt liquor and the fresh pack of UPLYFT he bought from the same store, Jaxon approached the grass at Beggar's Park. He planted himself on the green planks of the bench, squinting as he watched the sun set behind the high-rises of downtown like an underbite of broken fangs in front of a blinding fire. Jaxon was leaving himself vulnerable in such an exposed public space, but he wanted to be as far from distraction as possible – namely, his laptop. He sighed as he sat down, now aware that he couldn't inhabit his own bedroom without being seduced by that techno-window to the world, which sadly, he was now only using to commune with someone that no longer inhabited it.

He inhaled the brisk evening air as he reluctantly shoved the bright periwinkle tablet in his mouth.

Determined, he followed that tablet with another, then a pull from his bottle. Since he recently appeared immune to what LIFECAST Pharmaceuticals and Wellness deemed as the recommended dosage – two tablets no more than every six hours – he began popping them into his mouth like movie theater popcorn, as if it was merely a show about to unfold.

Jaxon felt that familiar tingling in his shoulders, accentuating a growing euphoria up his neck as he continued to roll them back in tiny circles. His head floated like a buoy in a calm yet unsettling ocean as he noticed the 16-dose package had just a few left. Satisfied he had consumed enough for the moment, he allowed his burdened head to recline backwards as the rest of his body oozed into molded comfort on the stiff bench.

His eyes fluttered closed.

BOOM!

A sound and force like a bomb, his whole being as the projectile shrapnel. Jaxon's periphery went black before a   glittery   spread   of   stars   faded   into   view ……...
....))))))))))))))))))))))))))))))))
)))
)))Oh)))my)))   God!)))   Finally))))))someone)))   was)))
open!))))))) Jaxon?)))))))))))))))))))))))))))))

He opened his eyes to Skye, his dearly departed friend who remained dear, though appeared no longer departed.

Past Skye.

She stood there looking at him, smiling, though frustrated as she through her hands up.

)))))Jaxon!)))

)))

((((Skye?((
((((((((((((((((((((((((((((((((((((((

))))Yeah)))))it's)))me))))Kind)))of))))Sorry)))this)))pla
ce)))is)))a)))mess))))))))))))))))))))))

She put another record on her turntable.

))))You)))know))))))I)))don't)))even)))want)))any)))of)
))this)))stuff)))))))))))))))))))))))))))))))She   motioned   to   her
albums.

))))I'm)))just)))using)))it)))because)))it's)))all)))still))))
here)))))for)))some)))reason)))))))))))

Jaxon's sight came into sharper focus. All her
possessions lay faded, scattered over this dark room, which
appeared a virtual negative film roll of her once vibrant
apartment. No posters or scotched-taped photo collages of
her and their friends on the walls – just different shapes in
varying shades of hue inside a pitch-black cube of
indeterminate size where only their bodies were illuminated.

((((Uh((((Skye(((((How((((((((((are(((you(((((((((((((
(((((((((((((((((((((((((((((((((((((

The closer he walked towards the wall, the wider its
angles fanned out, ever expanding into further darkness.

)))))Uh))))))I)))mean)))))I'm)))fine)))))I)))guess))))))
We)))don't)))really)))do)))that)))here)))
though)))
))))))))))))))))))))))))))))))))))

(((((Don't(((do(((what((((((((((((((((((((((((((((((((((
(((((((((((((((((((((((((((((((((((((

)))))You)))know)))))like)))))))))))))))))))))))))))))))))))))e
motion)))))))))))))))))))))))))))))))

(((((What((((((((do(((you(((mean((((((((((((((((((((((((
(((((((((((((((((((((((((((((((((((((

The question was delivered with slight surprise – he
realized he hadn't given her the hug he vowed to give if he

ever saw her again. In paralytic awe, those synapses wouldn't fire.

)))))What)))do)))I)))mean)))))I)))mean)))that's)))why)))I'm)))stuck)))here)))))Too)))much)))emotion)))))Too)))mu ch)))information)))))You)))guys)))won't)))let)))me)))go)))))*Y ou*)))))))))))

Jaxon)))))won't)))let)))me))go)))))))))))))))))))))))))))))))))))))

(((((But(((((*you're*(((the(((one(((that(((left(((us(((((Skye (((((You(((left(((us(((no(((choice(((but(((*to*(((let(((you(((go((((((((

)))))I'm)))sorry)))))But)))in)))order)))to)))really)))let)))me)))go)))))I)))actually)))need))) you)))to)))release)))me)))))Allow)))me)))to)))be)))dead)))))Th at's)))what)))I've)))been)))trying)))to)))tell)))you)))all)))this))) time))))))

(((((All(((((((((((((((((((((((((this(((((((((((((((((((((((((time(((((((((

)))))You're)))telling)))me)))you)))didn't)))hear)))me)))or))))))at)))least)))like)))))*feel*))) me)))speaking)))to)))you)))when)))you))were)))staring)))at)))me)))through)))your))) screen)))for)))the)))past)))two)))weeks)))))))))))))))))))))))))))))))))))))))))

(((((Well(((((I(((did(((notice(((that(((no(((matter(((ho w(((many(((times(((I(((saw(((a (((photo(((of(((you(((((or(((anything(((resembling(((you(((on (((your(((LIFECAST(((account(((((the(((worse(((I(((felt(((((((((((((((((

)))))Yes)))))exactly)))))That)))was)))me)))telling)))you)))to)))leave)))me)))alone)))))that)))you))were)))doing)))it)))

wrong)))))I)))swear)))))this)))has)))felt)))like)))screaming)))at)))a)))
massive)))crowd)))who)))claim)))they)))are)))there)))for)))m e)))))but)))their)))own)))chatter)))
drowns)))me)))out))))))even)))though)))it's))) *me*)))they're)))tr ying)))to)))recapture)))))))))))))))))))

She paused, staring at him straight in the eye, but careful not to expose too much it because any semblance of passion might confuse her message.

)))))That's)))what)))it)))feels)))like)))))))))))like)))I'm))) captured)))))))))))))Stuck(((

They stood in momentary silence. She knew he needed time for it to sink in. She felt a shadow of pity, considering he didn't know that these weren't real words she was talking with, just his interpretation of her consciousness, her sending signals.

But it seemed to be working.

((((((Can(((I(((ask(((what(((you(((meant(((when(((you (((said(((((Finally(((someone(((is(((open((((((((((((((((((((((((((((((((((((((((

)))))Sure)))))It's)))a)))little)))complex)))))so)))please)))try)))to)))keep)))up))))))))))))))))

Past Skye fought to find consistency to her drone so he could interpret it as Earth words –it was no longer her natural way of communicating.

)))))In)))a)))way)))))it's)))natural)))you)))all)))commu ne)))with)))me)))through)))the)))
LIFECAST)))Observer)))))where)))a)))lot)))of)))our)))share d)))memories)))are)))))how)))you)))
prefer)))to)))remember)))me)))))But)))we)))don't)))get)))the)))same)))satisfaction)))on)))the)))

other)))side)))))here)))))We)))can)))see)))you)))crying)))))havi
ng)))that)))catharsis)))))but)))we)))can't)))really)))respond))))
)That's)))because)))emotion)))is)))an)))Earthbound)))constr
uct)))))made)))only)))to)))interpret)))one)))another's)))vibrat
ions)))))Since)))web)))technology)))is)))new)))on)))Earth)))))
a)))lot)))of)))us)))are)))fastened)))here)))on)))the)))rim)))of)))
the)))drain)))))if)))you)))will))))))))))))))))))))trying)))to)))tell)))y
ou)))to)))stop)))occupying)))us)))so)))we)))can)))pass)))over)
))properly)))))Here)))))look)))))))))))))))))))))))))))))))))

Past Skye took Jaxon by the hand and led him to the
wall. A window appeared, offering a view of endless rows of
other black cubes suspended in black void just like hers.
Now in context, the view of this totality resembled an
endless battalion of fallen dominoes.

)))))Here)))))come)))closer)))))))))))))))))))))))))))))))))))))))
))

Jaxon squinted his eyes, focusing on each cube's
contents. Each one was inhabited by another Past version of
a departed body, screaming at portions of pixelated data.
Some were trying to talk sense into whoever was on the other
side. Others were in the throes of abandonment, giving up
their own ghosts. It was hard to watch, so he took a step
back to process.

)))))I)))know)))this)))is)))a)))lot)))))but)))I)))think)))y
ou're)))getting)))it)))))The)))toughest)))part)))is)))that)))we)))
can't)))blame)))you)))because)))you)))are)))basically)))lookin
g)))at)))))well)))))our)))interface)))))But)))we)))also)))*have*)))t
o)))blame)))you)))))because)))you're)))making)))this)))harder
)))on)))us)))than)))you)))can)))imagine)))))You))))see)))it)))as
)))empathy)))))as)))connection)))))when)))it's)))actually)))a)))
selfish)))gesture)))))Imagine)))a)))doctor)))refusing)))to)))cut
)))your)))umbilical)))cord)))))just))))))))))))))))))))))))))))))))))))
)))staring   at   you   while   you
scream((

(((((So(((((why(((me(((((Skye(((((How(((was(((I(((the(
((one(((you(((were(((able(((to(((

get(((through(((to((
((

)))))Well)))))there's)))two)))factors)))here)))and)))the
y're)))both)))difficult)))for)))me)))

to)))say)))to)))you))
)))

(((((Why((
((

)))))Okay)))))one)))))I'm)))not)))condoning)))it)))))b
ut)))you)))nearly)))consumed)))the)))

same)))overdose)))of)))UPLYFT)))that)))I)))did)))))You're))
)lucky)))to)))be)))alive)))))Your)))

saving)))grace)))is)))that)))you)))didn't)))shoot)))it)))up)))like
)))I)))did)))))Like)))an)))idiot)))))But)))I'm)))grateful)))you)))
had)))the)))guts)))to)))make)))a)))bridge)))to)))me)))like)))thi
s)))))

so)))I)))thank)))you))
)))

(((((Okay(((((And(((the(((second(((((((((((((((((((((((((((((
(((

)))))Don't)))make)))me)))say)))it)))Can)))we)))just)))
move)))on))

(((((Please(((((Skye(((((((((((If(((I'm(((gonna(((help(((y
ou(((((I(((need(((to(((know(((this((((((((((((((((((((((((((((((((((
(((
((((

))))Well)))))it)))was)))because)))of)))that)))one)))time
)))

(((((What(((one(((time(((
((

)))))Please)))don't)))make)))me)))spell)))it)))out)))))T
hat)))one)))night)))at)))my)))

apartment)))when)))we))
))))))you know)))))))))))))))))))))))))

(((((Sure(((((I've(((never(((forgotten(((it(((((Skye(((((
Why(((can't(((you(((say(((it(((out(((
loud(((
((((((((((((((((((((((((((((((((((((((

)))))Because)))we)))have)))to)))unlearn)))emotion))))
)graduate)))from)))information)))here)))in)))order)))to)))pas
s)))on))))))If)))I)))expose)))myself)))too)))much)))then)))may
be)))you)))will)))too)))))then)))it)))will)))be)))my)))fault)))if)))
you)))can't)))go)))back)))))   I)))can't)))do)))
that)))to)))you))
)))))))))))))))))))))))))))))))))

It took all her strength to contort her face back to
stoic. Realizing that she may have expressed too much anger,
the pendulum threatened to swing to the opposite extreme.

(((((Skye(((((this(((sounds(((like(((the(((same(((excus
es(((you(((were(((making(((back(((
when(((you(((were(((alive(((((back(((when(((you(((couldn't(((
handle(((your(((own(((feelings((
((
((((

She locked eyes with him, making sure he could see
her tears welling up, yet refusing to go into full sobs.

(((((Skye(((((just(((tell(((me(((what(((you(((want(((((
What(((do(((you(((need(((me(((to(((
do(((now(((that(((you(((have(((me(((here(((alone((((((((((((((((((
(((((((((((((((((((((((((((((((((((((

Nodding her head thoughtfully, she wiped a tear
away in spite of her dormant urge for exposure.

(((((C'mon((((((((((((If(((there's(((anything(((you(((nee
d(((me(((to(((relay(((((make(((it(((
quick(((((I(((think(((I(((feel(((a(((window(((back(((((((((((((((((((
(((((((((((((((((((((((((((((((((((((((

She leaned over to him and began whispering. It started in plain English before dissolving into a monotonous sustain

....

....

"Jaxon! Jaxon, wake up, bro! You there?

Marco was leaning over him on the bench at the park, slapping him lightly on the cheeks to make him come to. His eyes wouldn't open, but his mouth began to speak.

Her email. Her password.

"Delete it immediately. All of it. Fast. Please!" he whispered faintly.

Confused and worried how ghastly intoxicated Jaxon was, Marco still took the orders as gospel. He took out his phone and began thumbing his way into Skye's LIFECAST account, occasionally one-handing it as he put his arm around Jaxon for warmth. Marco shuddered, the way Jaxon's mouth kept opening and shutting like he was speaking somewhere else, to someone else.

He saw Jaxon's lips begin to pucker, his tongue emerging through his undulating lips as it licked the night air. His breathing got heavy, culminating with an amorous moan then...

One last breath from Jaxon Baker's Earth body.

Back in the cube the two became one, then became none, then became everything always in all time, as the remedial images of their human forms dissolved, no longer obligated to illustrate themselves to those they left behind.

Dear Diana Ranswell (Mom)

This is going to sound strange and please don't take it the wrong way but... You know how people sometimes will start their letters with "I hope this gets to you safely"? Well, I actually hope this letter doesn't get to you at all. Let me explain (God I really hope you don't have to end up reading this and I can just tell you all about it in person). And if anyone should read this before my Mother – may this letter serve as my alibi for this gruesome scene I regret you had to see here.

First of all, Mom – I just want you to know that you were totally right about Corey. I should have listened to you all along and now I'm paying the price, praying to make it out of this. I'm lying here somewhere just outside of Bear Creek getting slowly baked by the sun. I'm not sure where, exactly. We were looking to get out to the middle of nowhere, but every time I said "what about here? This looks good!" he just kept driving.

But that's the thing – now I AM in the middle of nowhere and Corey is dead five feet away from me. I'm wearing nothing but my jean shorts and cowboy boots because I have my T-shirt soaking up all the blood I'm losing out of my leg. I was wearing a bra, but I had to tie it around my thigh to make a tourniquet because Corey is such a bad shot.

Can you believe he did this? I know for a fact he's never shot a gun before – now look! Sorry, I forgot you can't. And I hope you won't. And I hope the next time you see me

I'll have just a limp and a tragic story to tell, because I swear to God I'm never coming out here again.

I had a feeling Corey was taking me on a trip to propose to me. That's why I didn't tell you where I was going, because I knew you never liked him. It pains me to realize it's been three months since you and I have talked. I'm so sorry, Mom. Him and I have had a lot of those 'now or never' talks lately. And when I say him and I, it was more like him saying it's now or never, over and over.

So, preparing myself for him to pop the question, I had written a poem for him in my journal here, to let him down easy. To let him know I loved him, but there were too many things that made me nervous about spending the rest of my life with him.

I thought it was weird that he didn't bring water if he knew we were going on a hike? He brought that fucking acoustic guitar instead. He just kept walking ahead of me singing this sad song "Nothin'" by Townes Van Zandt. This should have been the first red flag – he wasn't even singing it to me. But I guess in a way he was.

He was being so secretive about what we were doing or where we were even going. I just let him do his thing because I thought he was being romantic. Mysterious, you know? That's why I fell in love with him. Enough to even listen to him when he demanded we leave our cell phones in the car. To "unplug and be present," he said. But I didn't feel scared until I realized how thirsty I was, until I saw that we were way the fuck out here. I couldn't see the road anymore. But I guess he knew it would take all the water in the world when he'd be burning in Hell, so why bother with any at all?

But the thing is, Mom – I think *I'm* in Hell as well, only I'm wide awake. I just don't know what I did to deserve this. All I said was no. Then I panicked and told him I'd think about it because he started to get angry. That's when he took out his gun. Mom, I was thinking about you when I told him no. I just want you to know that.

But saying I had to think about it wasn't good enough for him, of course. Because he preferred that I don't think. He never liked that I had a mind of my own, and you saw that. Thank you, Mom. Even if it's too late.

He thought he had it all planned out. If I said no, which I pretty much did, he would kill me, then kill himself.

We started that morning at a bar. He just kept ordering shots with his beers. Ugh, he was drinking that disgusting peanut butter flavored whiskey nobody likes and now I can't get that taste out of my mind.

He kissed me on the way out, his tongue the last thing in my mouth.

He was still wasted when we started the hike, and I was just buzzed enough to fail seeing something was a little off. I can see now that he needed liquid courage to follow through with all of this.

But what a fucking moron. As if I wouldn't start running when he raised the gun up at me? So I ran and he just shot me once – got me in the back of my thigh, luckily. But Mom, it's taking every ounce of me to not think that maybe I would have been luckier if he had just killed me quick, instead of me just slowly baking and bleeding to death out here.

Mom, more than anything I wish I could say that was all. But there's more.

About ten minutes after Corey blew his brains out, I heard something that sounded like motorcycles. I was relieved it was some locals out there that heard the gunshot, so I started screaming for help so they would know where to go, because I'm on my back here hidden behind a big rock pile that look like all the other ones.

They found me. It was three guys, maybe in their

twenties, riding those white-trash ATVs. I started crying harder, just so relieved... but then they started laughing, Mom. Like, howling as if it was a joke. They were so drunk they could barely stand. They stumbled over to Corey and just started poking at him, at the hole in his head.

"Holy John F. Kennedy... Yup, he's dead! Cold fucking corpse!" one of them said, cracking up, while another one came and grabbed my chest.

"Whelp, this one is still nice and warm!" he yelled, all fucking excited. He kneeled over me just repeating that, saying I was nice and warm. I screamed as loud as I could. I uncrossed my arms just so I could reach into the back of my shorts where I was hiding Corey's gun, which I grabbed just in case some coyotes or bears smelled all this blood.

I shoved it in the guy's mouth and blew his brains out, Mom. Your daughter is now a murderer. How do you like that? But not just once – three times, cause the other two ran over to do God knows what to me so I shot them too. I guess this means I'm a better shot than Corey. *A Girl's Gotta Do What A Girl's Gotta Do*, right? I remember how much you loved that song when I was a kid.

What would you have done, Mom?

So, I have Corey's dead body five feet from my head, and these three, like, *Deliverance* motherfuckers spread like a pitchfork at my feet, but kind of angled out. So if I am lucky enough to get a search helicopter overhead, they're gonna see five people lying in the shape of a fucking peace sign. I just pray they don't think we're just some hippies trying to be cute out here.

My only saving grace is that I see the sun is finally going down, but that also means it's going to get cold. I can already feel my sunburnt skin throbbing with the temperature change. I'm thinking that someone has to come looking for these three guys. But it's my fault they never went home today. That they're never going home again. But if their family or friends do show up, how are they going to believe me when I tell them what really happened? They might just try to kill me anyway once they see they're all dead.

I guess that's why I'm writing this, so there will be no mystery.

I just checked the magazine in this .45 and there's two bullets left. I hate to think of what I might have to do with them. I'm so fucking hungry I can't even tell you. I didn't eat breakfast when I could have. I sort of lost my appetite at the bar because I saw how Corey was getting. But now I could eat anything. I'm scared to close my eyes, but I don't know what to do other than try to sleep, to speed up the chances of someone finding me. Us, I guess. Also, if I'm sleeping, I won't be hungry, right?

Mom, I'm so sorry for what I'm about to tell you. I hope one day you can see me as the same daughter you had before we stopped talking, before I found myself in these depths of unspeakable depravity. Unspeakable because I vow to never discuss aloud of what I have just done, but I need to document just how bad it has gotten here. Writing in my journals always made me... no, MAKES me feel better, no matter how tough life gets. So I can only hope these next few paragraphs will prove some semblance of catharsis – at the least, mirror back to me the shock of what has happened, to keep my blood flowing, because now it's getting freezing. I'm curled up in fetal position, wearing Corey's jacket as I write this.

So, I managed to get some sleep at least, but I'm not sure how long because time has become very abstract here. I woke up not just because I was shivering – I felt a hunger. An emptiness that quickly became a nauseating pain that nearly rivaled my gunshot wound.

I looked at Corey, wondering what's the point of

wearing so many layers when you're dead. Earlier today I thought it was stupid he was wearing his fringe suede jacket in 112 degree heat, but now I'm so grateful that he did. I managed to get the strength to scoot myself up to him. It took a long time, but I was able to position his arms up in order to slip the jacket off. It's a big jacket, so it actually covers up some of my wound as well. I stopped shivering for a while, but then I did something that made me start to panic and now I can't tell if I'm shaking because I'm cold or because of the thought of what I've done.

Before I slipped the jacket off Corey, I looked at his face. The moon was shining bright enough where I could make out his features. Finally, he looked at rest. Lovingly, I touched his head, I guess to sort of say my last goodbye. My hand went into his exit wound, and I saw about a quarter of his skull was blown off. It was moist, all blood and brain, so my hand got all covered in Corey. Before I could reason how or why, my hand just went right to my tongue. I licked the blood off. It ignited my hunger and was also quenching my thirst. Before I knew it, I just kept going until my hand was clean.

But I know I will never be truly clean again. I went back for more, somehow having the courage to chew. I found some of what I think was his brain matter, making sure there was no hair in it. It just went right into my mouth, Mom. I nibbled at first, just to see if I could handle the taste. It went right down, easier than I thought, little by little. Before I knew it, my hand was going in for seconds. I was able to keep it down, too, and the pain in my stomach went away. Corey made me try *tacos de sesos* once, even though it was the last thing I wanted to do at the time. So, this isn't that much different, I guess. His dead body isn't doing any good just lying there attracting flies, so I guess a girl's gotta do what a girl's gotta do.

And that's all I got for now, Mom.
See you soon, I hope.
Love always,
Allysa.

Wrath Child's Atrophy

Jeremy didn't realize what a quiet Saturday afternoon it was until he took off his headphones. Side-A of Dark Angel's *Darkness Descends* cassette clicked off his Walkman, revealing a muted atmosphere in contrast to the high-volume thrash metal delicacy he was indulging in. His ears perked up. Perplexed, he initially assumed he was hearing the hissing of a tape already finished, only to realize it was his parents whispering downstairs.

Why would they be whispering? he thought. He took it as a cue to listen closer. If they didn't want him to hear it, it was likely something about him. He opened his door, which was already slightly ajar, before approaching the top of the staircase, well hidden from their view from the kitchen.

"I feel like we should tell him. What if he knows something?"

"It's not quite cause for alarm yet. It's only been twenty-four hours."

"Yeah, but there was a long, cold night in that twenty-four hours."

"Are you afraid of what you might hear if you ask him?"

Then he heard the name David. *Were they talking about Davey Rothchild?*

Davey went by Wrath Child to his friends –the older teenage Hessian gang The Heathens, who Jeremy and his pals looked up to. A few of them were their older brothers. But Jeremy, an eleven-year-old only child still trying to grow his hair out like the older heavy metal kids, saw their leader Davey as the cool, cigarette-smoking big brother he wished he had.

The Heathens were only three years older, yet a gaping chasm of vice, experience, and bad reputation would prevent any chance of the boys getting to hang with the denim-clad demons.

Jeremy's reverence of Davey was equaled by a substantial fear, as rumors ran about his involvement in Devil worship; though many would claim the Anton LaVey scribed *Satanic Bible* he always kept in his back pocket was just for shock value. Either way, it was an effective accessory.

"Jeremy, please come downstairs! We need to speak with you."

Startled, he gave himself ten seconds before descending so they wouldn't know he was that close. He heard nearly everything. A mild anxiety overtook him, knowing he had to hear it again and would have to act surprised, shocked.

"By any chance, have you seen David Rothchild since Thursday?"

"Um, no. I mean, how would I? You guys don't let me hang out with him," he said, unable to hide a mild bitterness.

"Because he always reeks of marijuana, Jeremy! And guess what? He's missing. They've called the police and everything. Do you have any idea where he could have gone? None of his friends seem to know anything so Richard and Pam are encouraging all the parents to ask their own kids, regardless. It's such a small town, you know."

"Okay," he said, solemnly. "Do Tommy and Chris know yet?"

"We're not sure, but you should give them a call since they're your closest friends."

Jeremy didn't rush to the phone, exactly. Instead, he went semi-catatonic with wonder, his imagination running wild with what kind of backwoods mayhem The Wrath Child was chasing. He was concerned, but not surprised. He felt obligated to hide his excitement. Davey Wrath Child was already a legend, so this just made sense –with him disappearing and everyone talking about him with this kind of sensationalism.

He called Tommy and Chris on three-way. They had already heard, so they devised to meet at the park.

***

They showed up in similar uniforms – blue jeans and their favorite heavy metal T-shirts. Tommy in his Judas Priest, Chris in his Metallica, and Jeremy in his King Diamond tee that he never took off. It was like a sports team with their sacred numbered jerseys.

"So, what do you guys think?" asked Jeremy.

"This is really sketchy, man," Chris said, shaking his head. "My brother said Wrath Child was talking all kinds of crazy stuff lately. He's really into this thing called the *Necronomicon*, which is this satanic book where even if you look at it, you get possessed by the Devil. And I guess he's got a copy somehow?"

"Woah!" Jeremy and Tommy exclaimed, but Jeremy's excitement came with a tightening stomach.

"Oh shit. That's not good, I saw that in the *Evil Dead*! *The Book of the Dead*, it's called. I didn't think it was real."

"Do you guys think Wrath Child is dead? Like, what if he sacrificed himself like he always talked about?"

"No way, he's the toughest guy on Earth! I could picture him fighting demons at the end of the world. Like, he's so evil I bet the Devil would even be scared of him!"

The other two agreed. He was definitely still alive, but maybe he transported himself into another world using one of those spells? Davey would often talk in a warped backwards speech to freak people out, claiming he was hexing you. He would follow it with his crazy laugh that was almost as scary as the whole talking backwards thing.

"And you know, those guys are only fourteen and they get wasted. They drink beer and vodka and smoke marijuana, but I guess Wrath smokes it like cigarettes, one after the other… My brother was telling me he even was kind of worried about him, cause his eyes have been all, like, big and red and veiny and stuff," said Chris. "Like, he looks scary now without even meaning to."

"Like how people in the movies look when they get possessed?" asked Jeremy.

"Yeah, yeah like that!"

The boys were just as much elated as they were terrified by what was coming out of their own mouths, proving fear was merely the shadow side of fascination. They traded mythic theories, amped-up fantasies about what they hoped was Davey's fate during this detour of inter-dimensional purgatory. Jeremy claimed he went out to the forest, drew a big pentagram in the dirt and was teleported to Hell. Chris heard that marijuana was also sometimes called 'Devil's Lettuce' and so maybe the weed transported him into some kind of wicked Netherworld. Tommy took the Earthbound theory, that he stole a car and crashed it, yet was okay, but was also probably in jail. But one thing they all agreed on – that Davey would be back soon to tell them all about it. The Wrath Child would return victorious, even if they'd have to secretly meet up with him to hear about his adventures and never tell their parents.

As the sun went down, the boys began to run out of material as the gravity of the situation really began to weigh on them.

"But, what if he never comes back?" asked Jeremy. "Like, who would take his place as the leader of The

Heathens?"

"Probably my brother, that's his best friend," said Chris. "Then, next thing you know, I'll be in The Heathens, then I'll get you guys in there!"

"Yeah, but I don't want The Wrath Child to go away forever," mourned Tommy. "Like, I'd rather just have him back rather than join The Heathens if it was either-or."

They went silent, experiencing the sinking feeling of pre-pubescent helplessness, like they were sort of lost themselves. They weren't the cops, they were just kids. What could they do?

"Well, we've got to do something!" said Jeremy. "I mean, if Davey did a satanic ritual to disappear, maybe we could do one to bring him back?"

"Ok, but we don't know anything about that stuff," said Chris.

"Listen, I never told anyone this," Tommy began. "But this one time The Wrath Child was with my brother at our house. My brother's door was open just a crack, and I saw them both in there blasting metal. The room was all smoky and they were sitting with their eyes closed. The Wrath Child sensed me there though, 'cause he opened his eyes and started yelling at me that they were doing witchcraft to get girlfriends. Did you know you could do that?"

"Woah, so your brother is into it too?" Jeremy asked.

"I dunno, that's the first I ever saw him get weird like that."

"Okay, I've got it!" Jeremy exclaimed. "My parents are leaving me alone tomorrow night. I think they're seeing a movie so we'll only have two hours to do this…"

Jeremy went was giddy as he hashed out the plan. His parents' movie was at seven PM, so Tommy and Chris would leave their houses right when he saw them pull out of the driveway. Tommy knew where his brother stored his weed, so he would pinch the tiniest bit, so small he wouldn't notice. This would be the first time they had smoked, so it would double as a coming-of-age initiation.

Jeremy knew this one King Diamond song, "Welcome Home." They would play it over and over as they got stoned, concentrating on a mental image of The Wrath Child, visualizing his return. Tommy had the same cassette as well, so he would bring his boom box and they would synch up both Jeremy's stereo and the boom box, which would be on his windowsill, pointing outside into the night sky so maybe The Wrath Child could hear it, wherever he might be!

They would beckon him back. Especially so the crummy cops would be off his trail, they thought. The Wrath Child didn't need that kind of heat.

***

Tommy and Chris arrived on time with their watches synched. The three didn't say much, treating it as a solemn, determined ceremony too much overthinking might dilute. Besides, they were each a tad nervous to try marijuana for the first time by themselves. Each one of them envisioned their first time being administered by The Wrath Child himself, finally showing them the ropes from an intimate proximity.

Tommy brought a substantial nug. *How are we gonna smoke this?* they asked, a vital detail overlooked. They didn't have a pipe, rolling papers, or even any apples they could core out. But paper is paper, they thought, as they tore off a piece of yellow paper from a legal pad, cutting it into a three by three-inch square. They ground the green into a fine dust, enough to roll the jaundiced joint, sealing it tight with a glue stick they found in Jeremy's mom's craft drawer. After they found matches by the fireplace, they were poised and ready as they walked upstairs to Jeremy's room.

Both Jeremy and Tommy were armed with their King Diamond *Them* cassettes, both meticulously cued to the second track, "Welcome Home."

"Ready?"

"Ready."

They inserted each tape, one into the ghetto blaster sitting precariously on the open window, the other safely into Jeremy's bedroom stereo.

"Now."

They both pressed play as Chris lit the end of their homespun drug vessel. The opening drum fill served as a wake-up call to arms, to bring back their estranged, if not vicarious, comrade. The operatic vocals called into the black of night, its eternal shadows becoming one with Jeremy's bedroom now that he had hit the lights.

"BROTHAAAAAAA, WELCOME HOME!!!" they heard King Diamond wail.

Chris took a hearty toke, inhaling with mature gusto. He passed it to Jeremy, who then passed it to Tommy, each one trying to outdo one another with how long they held the smoke in. As a virgin euphoria filled their fibers, their minds swayed like wheat in the wind, seduced by the theatrical splendor of a song they just knew would bring back The Wrath Child. As the high rose, their knees got weak, drawing them to the ground where they assumed the same cross-legged position Tommy had witnessed Davey and his brother in. He made sure Jeremy and Chris did it just like him, just like he remembered. They felt a power in their conspiracy, a righteous occult solidarity, as much as they felt a heaviness pulling them down further.

By the end of the song, they were fast asleep. It wasn't so much that it was great weed as much as it was just decent glue stick.

**

Jeremy was the first to wake up a quarter past nine. He panicked, knowing his folks would be home any minute. Luckily, the wind had picked up, wafting the smell of weed out the window, an aromatic smoke signal to The Wrath Child. The gusts were flexing harder, billowing air under Jeremy's posters with such force it looked like they might tear off the tacks.

"Guys, wake up!" he whispered, shaking them out of their haze. "I think the Wrath Child is giving us a sign!"

The posters shook violently from the gale, as if his whole room had come alive.

"What do you think he's trying to tell us?" asked Chris.

"He's obviously telling us that he's still out there!" said Tommy.

"Yeah, but you guys gotta go, quick! My parents will be home any minute and I don't want them to wonder what we've been up to," said Jeremy, dictated by a slight wash of weed-induced paranoia.

Tommy and Chris climbed out the window and down the metal trellis. Tommy descended one-handed, the other tight on the handle of his boom box. Jeremy saw them high-five then take off running, ignited by the rush of unholy weather spiking their adrenaline.

**

The next day, Davey Rothchild was found in the middle of a cornfield on the outskirts of town, right by the Walmart where he was last seen. After scouring the area with local volunteers, the police found his young, lifeless body in a clearing that it appeared he made himself, crushing the stalks with his army boots, likely out of panic. His eyes were still open, bloodshot, mouth agape like a silent scream.

The coroners found marijuana and alcohol in his system. The theory was that he had been walking aimlessly in the corn, the tall stalks confusing his instinctual compass. As he went deeper into the field, it would all look the same to him, contributing to his disorientation. Add in the unforgiving Midwestern summer sun that often sneaks up on a person, and David Rothchild didn't stand a chance. He died from dehydration and exposure, his fourteen- year-old body not able to withstand the heat stroke that befell him.

***

Jeremy broke down in tears when his parents sat him down that Monday afternoon. At first, he refused to believe it; all those fantasies of Davey's return taking such strong hold in his, Chris's, and Tommy's minds. But there were too many details to deny, even for such fertile, unjaded imaginations as theirs.

Jeremy walked up to his room, not really knowing what to do other than listen to King Diamond again. He cued up "Welcome Home," already deciding it was The Wrath Child's memorial song ushering him into the beyond. He unfolded the cassette cover to read along with the lyrics.

"Wait, what?" he whispered to himself.

He never bothered to fully dissect the song until this moment. To his shock, the lyrics were nothing like what the boys heard in their heads.

"GRANDMAAAA!!! WELCOME HOME," his stereo speakers confirmed as he read along.

"Grandma?" he whispered.

"GRANDMAAAA?!?" he yelled. "This song is about King Diamond's goddamned grandma?"

He got on the phone and dialed Tommy's number, then got Chris on three-way.

"Guys," he began. "We fucked up…"

BAPTISM!

It was the last weekend of June. The high-noon desert sun had just begun to really make its presence known, as the weather went from bright with pleasant breeze to downright scorching in just ten minutes, as the last cloud dissipated above the Desert Hot Springs Spa Hotel. The DHSSH boasted a U-shaped hotel building that horseshoed eight pools of the conflicted, crime-ridden city's unique healing water, each one varying in degrees, capacity, and more fluidly, age. The hotter the pool, the more adults you may find there enjoying the mineral soak of their world-weary bones. The colder the pool, the rowdier children you'd find, as the hot pools felt like the chore of a bath. It was there in the cool water they would splash violently, Devil-may-care as if it was the ocean or your normal poorly supervised municipal pool.

Tommy and Aubrey were causing quite a stir in that one in the far-left corner, still covered in deep shade due to the fortunate position of the mid-day sun. Unattended, the boy and his younger sister's shrieking volume was viciously competing with the size of the waves they were making as they chased one another along the edges. This eventually created an uncomfortable whirlpool effect that had made their parents and the others exit minutes ago. Tommy and Aubrey took the mass exodus as a fine excuse to accelerate their spastic flailing and exclamations, truly claiming their autonomy in a quickly shortening summertime.

Aubrey finally caught her brother in the quick-turn of a counter-clockwise fake-out. Classic. Their laughter exploded upon the shock of their contact before quickly nose-diving, exhausted. She was relieved the game was over so she could finally catch her breath, her brother older, faster and often with more feral impulses.

"Okay, I'm gonna get out and rest now!" Aubrey declared.

"Oh, no you don't" interrupted Tommy as he grabbed her ankle. "We're not done yet! Now, we are going to play BAPTISM!!!"

Aubrey was over it. She rolled her eyes right into her head as Tommy yanked her back into the pool.

"Tommy!" she protested, thrashing her fists into the increasingly turbulent water.

She only got two feet away before Tommy grabbed her little bicep with one hand and her drippy pig-tailed head with the other.

"But you've never been baptized, Aubrey!"

Now with both hands on her head, Tommy dunked her all the way under the coldest water. He kept her down there with all his weight, one left leg on her shoulder, grimacing with the raw determination of impending victory.

Aubrey's eyelids peeled back, her corneas bulging as she could not hold her breath any longer. She even began to pray to God.

Kept Change

"It's all about the birds and bees/and where it all went wrong/and where it all belongs." – **Don Van Vliet**

As the Earth's surface continued to boil, swirl, crack, and freeze, we also grew uncomfortable in our skin. A palpable membrane of anxiety had replaced the Earth's atmosphere – by this time, global warming was considered one of those *vintage fears* that in theory, no longer existed. Yet, it survived due to its long-established damage – its permanent residence.

So, we remained indoors.

Back in 2019 no one would have thought the trendy blueprint of an apartment above the strip mall – once considered *live/shop/work spaces* – would be the mandatory model for future living in the present 2029.

From our apartments, we simply walk down a contained flight of stairs to our jobs among the variety of commerce. After work, we acquire essentials, then walk back up to continue our latest conquest of binge-watch on NOWTV. We nourish ourselves *and* get our steps in.

It's not just all-inclusive – it's all enclosed, in the same style of militaristic cube architecture that takes up each city block, so no one feels left out. One massive cube per block. If it appears oppressive from an outside perspective, all one has to do is consider all the life inside. Luckily, any outside perspective is limited to the drone surveillance system – machines that are the only intelligence privy to the fact that our world now resembles a boundless cemetery.

But still, somehow along the way, we've achieved the maximum limits of boredom. Despite seamless acclimation to the new security of our air-conditioned microcosms, we've nearly forgotten what it was like before, but also who we could have been.

Now that the planet has reached its *irreversible* status, its inhabitants – forever unsatisfied – have begun to focus on our own bodies to change.

To manipulate like a fad.

To pick at like a scab.

All in an effort to be reborn with our new world.

Since rendered unnecessary to leave our blocks, a shared phenomenon had befallen certain trailblazing citizens who feel a primal urge to leave their skin – or more specifically, their genders.

Life has, in fact, become sexless. For those coupled up, a night's climax in bed would be replaced by ceaseless searching through multiple episodes of the latest NOWTV series, stopping at nothing to reach *that* climax of each show's conclusion. While couples do this side by side on a sofa, it's the most intimate bonding they can radiate before falling asleep on their respective sides, remaining upright with strained necks like wilted flowers.

For the more adventurous singles, evenings are spent at the block's nightclub, typically located at the bottom end of the cube's maze-like descending path. The inconvenience of the club's location is by design – one is forced to pass every storefront before reaching its lonely, poorly attended corner at the lowest levels of the foundation. Often the single man or woman on the prowl arrives reluctantly with a handful of shopping bags. Realizing how awkward it is not to have a free hand, they turn around and walk all the way back to their apartment.

Alone again.

But not this time – not this Saturday night, thought Kevin Marcus, who lived on the third level of the 1021st Block. Kevin was on a mission for action at his block's bar *Destiny*

Gambol. He felt a profound momentum, successfully avoiding temptation as he walked past popular men's stores like WEAR-WOLF, THE SHOE FLY, and BEER ME!, the craft liquor store where he worked. He was hoping he might see the attractive brunette from level six again, maybe find the courage to ask her something else besides the floor she lived on, and this time hopefully without a handfuls of impulse items.

Kevin blew into the dimly lit Destiny Gambol like a breeze. He scanned the crowded room. *Wow, place is packed, though I've never seen these people before. Must be new tenants, but all at once? And have these people all taken the same confidence-boosting drug? They're having the time of their lives! They're all grooving in synch, like they all know each other already but I don't know, they look a little... off?*

Typically, Kevin would fall victim to self-inflicted alienation when faced with anyone having too much fun. But this uninhibited display was contagious.

He got right in there, continuing to scan for the brunette.

There she was. Dancing with a rather masculine woman. Or was it a very feminine man? No matter, it looked like she was uncommitted for now – just having fun, as he saw her cut in with another clubber, radiant with sexual-ambiguity. She swung her head as her dark bob flew away from her eyes, opening a view directly at Kevin.

She smiled.

She whispered something to her dance partner, rubbing their shoulder as she began to walk toward him.

"You're the guy from the other night, right?"

"Yeah, Kevin from level three! I never got your name?"

"Tracy. Tracy Noble," she replied, nodding her head warmly. "I was a little late getting the memo to what's going on here tonight – somehow I feel like you may be too?" she asked, staring inquisitively at the area that made him a man.

"Yeah, I was gonna ask…"

"Revolution, baby! All these people – these actually very *normal* people – are part of this whole thing, what they're calling a *Sex Clash Club Crash*. It's all regular people who trade their gender in for a night and see how the other half lives. It's kinda crazy but, I mean, look how much fun they're having?"

Now that he knew, Kevin re-scanned the room to assess. Hetero as he was, a wash of relief came over him, as he was whisked back to his younger days in Hollywood where he would cross dress.

He loved the anonymity of cross-dressing. He considered it a sort of tribute to women – because he truly *loved* women, along with their fashion. He even committed to wearing female undergarments. The underwear was his favorite indulgence – it wasn't just arousing, it made him feel, well, *pretty*.

"Hey," she nudged him. "You still there?"

"Ha! Yeah, sorry… Okay, listen. My name is Kevin and I know this is forward but I have a crazy idea."

Tracy's eyes lit up, praying it was what she thought.

"Oh my God I think I love it already…"

Kevin grabbed her hand, leading her out of the club as they started running through the shopping center back to his apartment. The thrill was all Tracy's as the lights of the storefronts whizzed by her. She already thought this guy was special – but the wild discipline of traversing the whole mall without buying anything?

They didn't need to. Once they entered Kevin's apartment, they had everything they needed. They began removing their clothing – frantic yet careful not to pop any buttons. Instead of throwing them on the floor, they handed each article right over one another – blue jeans for the black skirt, his white dress shirt for her black blouse, black brassiere for his white *wifebeater* undershirt, boxers for panties, nylons for socks.

"And… thank you." Kevin looked at her right in the eyes as she handed him her hosiery.

"Oh my God, thank *you*. Okay, can I do you now?"

Tracy whipped the make-up bag out of her purse. Within six masterful minutes Kevin's face popped like a Nagel painting. Returning the favor, Kevin took a baby wipe from his nightstand and went to work on her, removing her make up to reveal her natural untainted beauty. He handed her one of his Stetsons as she pulled her hair up. Her locks in a pile on her head made the hat fit nice and tight.

They returned downstairs, reeling from excitement of their new transformation, like something confined inside them had been turned loose. For Kevin, of course, it was a revisit to freedom. They re-entered Destiny Gambol instantly turning heads – inspiring applause, even – as their new crowd stood impressed at how quickly they caught up with their new social coup.

***

Kevin and Tracy proved inseparable. Within two whirlwind months they made a landmark decision to move in together. Kevin gave up his place on level three and elevated himself to her place on the sixth. They ended every night at Destiny Gambol, as Sex Clash Club Crash had since taken permanent residence there. No longer a fly-by-night community experiment, its influence had quickly spread not just to the other blocks but was now happening in every major city as a conscious alternative to the mundane.

NOWTV even saw its first dip in ratings – a

substantial percentage of *Sex Clashers* began to associate staying home and binge-watching with defeatist boredom and the old guard of disaffection.

It was a time of firsts for people like Kevin and Tracy as well. It was a Saturday night, and while Kevin was now the one who spent too much time in the bathroom applying his make-up, Tracy was mysteriously hogging it while he paced around impatiently. Before he could holler for the third time that they were going to be late, she dramatically kicked open the door, standing hands on hips, glaring at him with a freshly shaved head.

"Holy shit, honey! You look so cool!" She could do no wrong in his eyes.

"Ha! Thanks. I figured I should step it up since you bought the wig. You know, I was thinking – what if you changed your name? I mean, I'm Tracy, which can go either way. Kevin just sounds so unlike you anymore."

"Great point, Tracy. From now on, I'm Kylie. Always loved that name for a girl."

"Awesuuuum! I actually already got you the legal petition form. I put it on your desk while you were doing your make-up. See, I'm a man – *I get stuff done!*"

He did a double take, interrupting his smile with a bitten lip. "Thank you, baby. We're really going past the point of no return, aren't we?"

***

That night of firsts continued down at Destiny Gambol. Little did they know they'd be walking into an impromptu celebration for their friend Blair, who had just gone *all the way*. While a female to male sex change wasn't the rarest thing in the world anymore, it was the first time any of these new Destiny Gambol regulars had achieved it. Like the dawning of a new era where anything was possible.

"Honey, this would have gone down two years ago if it wasn't for the mandatory therapy! Puleeze! As if I don't know what I want and shouldn't get it *when* I want!" Blair replied after Tracy congratulated him for the perseverance.

Another first, and on an even more enigmatic note: it appeared Tracy was behaving far boisterously than usual. First, Kevin noticed she was making every single person high-five her – even doubling down on those caught off guard. Then, she was trying to bump chests with each person who happened to nod in agreement with her during conversation. But when they'd recoil in confusion, she would save it with another last-ditch high-five. Second, she was drinking far more than usual. She continued ordering shots and double-fisting beers, but this was clearly a *result of* the aggressive body contact language and not the other way around.

Third, she was referring to everyone as *bro* and *dude*, even slipping into a displaced Staten Island accent, even though she had lived on the West Coast her whole life. Kevin couldn't help but laugh – it was becoming absurd. But every time he would giggle, she would sock him in the chest.

Hard.

"Bitch!" she would say.

Kevin could take hits, but it was getting embarrassing. He resisted until he could no longer bear it, finally taking her aside.

"Hey, baby… Can I ask you something if you promise not to take it the wrong way?"

"Yo, what's up?" she responded with an arcane hip-hop hand gesture.

"Do you… actually know what it's like to be a man? Like, just a normal guy? I can't speak for all men, but it's not at all like how you're acting tonight."

Tracy's eyes became far away as she went silent, unresponsive even to Kevin's third attempt addressing her.

"Okay, let's get you home…" he said, as he tried in vain to put his arm around her. She walked ahead the whole way back as Kevin obediently trailed behind. The only moment they walked in synch was when they both noticed a group of hard hats putting the finishing touches on a new business opening, though indistinguishable, as they had just began applying the letters to their brand name marquee.

When they got back to their apartment, Kevin tried once again to pierce the disarming silence of her steely gaze.

"I… don't want to talk about it," she finally blurted out. "Yeah, maybe something happened to me years ago, but you're still a man under all that make-up, so you wouldn't get it. And it's none of your business."

Even with his ribs still throbbing from her unprovoked roughness earlier, these words were like a punch in his stomach. After all the intertwining intimacy they shared, she was suddenly a stranger. A profound sadness overwhelmed him while he scrambled for something, anything to save the evening on a decent note, maybe something they'd never done before.

"I know it sounds sort of mediocre, but why don't we just sit and watch NOWTV? We've never done that as a couple, and we need to just turn off our brains for a bit, I think?"

Tracy shrugged her shoulders as she sat on the couch. Kevin took this as a *yes* as he flipped on the big screen in front of them and joined her right in time for a commercial while they got comfortable.

A vanilla man and woman, both platinum blonde, appeared on the screen while a horrid Midi-horn version of Bowie's *Changes* played beneath their pitch.

Hi, I'm Greg!

And I'm Peggy!

(Together) And we'd like to welcome you to GREG AND PEGGY'S SPARE PARTS FOR BROKEN HEARTS, the world's first franchised walk-in gender fixer-upper!

"Wait, is this a show, or a commercial… or some kind of joke?" Kevin wondered out loud.

"It's obviously a commercial, Kylie," Tracy mumbled under her breath. "Remember you were too cheap to get the upgraded NOWTV with no commercials? Great, I think it's modeled after one of those vintage half-hour long infomercials too, in front of a rehearsed studio audience," she groaned, rolling her eyes as the invasive commercial raged on.

"Are you one of those people that, just, never felt comfortable in their own skin? Like you were born in the wrong body? Folks, in our ever-changing world we see the blur of progress practically erasing our histories, sometimes we can't remember what an old city block used to resemble, anymore than who WE used actually be. Can you remember, what used to make you YOU?"

"Well, if the answer is no, we've got good news for you: You're only human. These estranged feelings we get as we usher in the new world aren't just perfectly normal – they're EXCITING! There's a shift going on – a revolution – and here at Greg and Peggy's Spare Parts for Broken Hearts, we're getting in on the ground floor of this magic moment!

(YOUR MAGIC MOMENT! OUR MAGIC MOMENT! The audience screamed in unison*)*

"Folks, we feel that all the strife and conflict in our world, since the beginning of time, has been a result of The War of The Sexes – the eternal inability to truly empathize with the opposite sex, bringing those existential feelings of self-loathing that often result in aggression towards others. While we can't stop being human, what we have now are OPTIONS to take control and become somebody brand new… and while the practice has been around for quite some time, we've got a

patent on the most streamlined version of sex change technology, and we are calling it GENDERCIDE!

(APPLAUSE)

"Wait, did they just say Gendercide?" Kevin asked.

"Yeah, why?"

"Tracy, that's already a term. It has *nothing* to do with sex change. Gendercide is the systematic killing – you know, genocide – of members of a specific gender. Sort of like what happened to all those women in Juarez thirty years ago..."

"Oh, quit mansplaining, Kylie... I honestly don't even remember that ever happening and I doubt anyone would. Stop interrupting the infomercial, please?" Tracy was suddenly more focused on the TV than she had been with Kevin for the last month.

"That's right, Gendercide! Folks, let me ask you a question: Who made the decision what gender you were going to be? God? Your parents? SO-CI-YO-TEE?"

"Well, not YOU, that's for sure! Now, let me ask you another question. What IS gender? Is, like, that even a thing?"

(NOOOOOO!!!)

"Now, let's look at sex. Our so-called genders seem to have been revealed as a mass-conspiracy from the powers that be to procreate – to propagate our species. Well, guess what? No one is even having sex anymore! I mean, get with it, people! The writing is on the bedroom walls!"

"Sex. The old 'in-out,' right? Well, just because we are no longer having sex doesn't mean we can't get inside *each other anymore. With Gendercide, the 'getting inside' one another has taken on a whole new level of commitment!"*

(WOOOOOOW!!!)

"Now, you seem like a crowd that knows what they want when they want it, right?"

(YEEEEAAAHH!!)

"Well, the best part of Greg and Peggy's Spare Parts for

Broken Hearts is that there is no more waiting *with our newly patented hour-short Gendercide operation! Who says you have to spend two grueling pre-op years with some hack shrink making sure you really want what you really, really want?!?"*

(NO ONE!!!)

Within the span of the commercial, Kevin went from fascinated to disgusted.

"Broken hearts? This is trite, just fucking creepy. It's not as if every single one of us are broken people or something... I feel like these people are trying to profit from us, like co-opting our whole lifestyle. They're just creating more anxiety in people like us who happen to be more susceptible to it, in order to tap into our vulnerabilities, then right into our wallet. And I mean, look at this Greg and Peggy couple – they're as straight as they come!" he said, pointing to the screen.

Tracy said nothing, remaining transfixed to the screen.

"NOW I'VE GOT JUST ONE LAST QUESTION FOR YOU, STUDIO AUDIENCE... WHAT SIDE ARE YOU ON?!?"

(GENDERCIDE!!!)

"THAT'S RIGHT!!! Now, can we have a volunteer..."

"Alright, I've had enough. You want to get ready for bed?" Kevin looked forward to slipping into his nightgown, thankful to have a partner like Tracy who understood these little things about him.

"No, I'm good. I've gotta see how they do this..."

***

The next night, as the regular crowd assembled at Destiny Gambol, Kevin opted to stay home while Tracy joined them solo. He thought he might change his approach – this time, to challenge her new abrasive personality with nothing but kindness and hospitality. After she left for the bar, he snuck downstairs to GROCERY ISLE, their block's new Tiki-themed food market, to grab some quick ingredients to make them a candle-lit late-night dinner when she got home. He was giddy, brimming over with anticipation of her surprise.

On his way back to the apartment, Kevin noticed the new storefront they passed the previous night had just opened that day. A grand opening, it appeared. For a split second he was amazed at their progress. Two seconds later he filled with dread, peering up to the sign above the glass windows.

GREG AND PEGGY'S SPARE PARTS FOR BROKEN HEARTS.

GRAND OPENING FULL SERVICE SPECIAL – $100!!!

OPEN TWENTY-FOUR HOURS SEVEN DAYS A WEEK!

He nearly fainted at the sight. What was one of the most surreal nightmares he had watching a television commercial was now a reality.

Now, he had to believe it.

Another sign boasted all of their other locations at nearly every other block in a ten-city radius, like a Starbucks for the sex change set.

He walked faster, back to the confines of his apartment, which was in the confines of the shopping center, in the confines of the block, and so on. He got to his door, fumbling with the keys as he raced inside. He nervously started chopping meat, then unwrapped the vegetables, forgetting every ten seconds exactly what he was doing and why he was doing it.

An hour passed and Kevin had successfully gotten everything into the oven. He knew Tracy would be home around ten since it was a work night, so all he had to do was re-heat the casserole dish if it finished early and she wasn't home yet.

He waited. It was now 10:16 and there was no sight of her, no text from her appearing on the NOWTV screen where he was watching the World War Three special on the History Channel, just to pass the time.

10:47. He was starting to get worried. He texted her twice and even tried calling. No response.

It was now eleven. He began to pick at the food, starving as he gingerly stuck a fork into the dish in the oven to tide him over.

11:30 came and he was in a cold sweat, wondering if he should just get into his nightgown and call it a night, when Tracy opened the door. He felt dizzy with relief as he ran to the door, his arms outstretched to embrace her.

"Don't fucking touch me!" she screamed as she recoiled. "Don't you dare fucking touch me!"

She had changed again. Kevin's mouth dropped as he tried to push words out, but he could muster nothing but a sad stutter.

"You cookin'? Smells like you're cookin', but I don't see my damn food anywhere…"

She pushed him aside as she walked past, following the smell into the kitchen. Kevin in pursuit, frantic and on the verge of tears.

He began apologizing, he wasn't sure why.

"Shut up! Just shut the hell up and why am I coming home to a messy kitchen?"

Kevin shook his head in disbelief, his legs weak. He felt a gravity beckoning him to crumble into the linoleum, but he finally found the words through his tears.

"Wha… why are you acting like this? You know this isn't how we act, right? Where are you getting this fro…"

And before he could finish, Tracy's open hand came swinging down on his cheek, a force like a Louisville Slugger that knocked him to the floor.

She pointed at him, now curled up fetal, trembling in hysteric synch with his own sobbing.

"You. Don't tell me. What it's like to be a man. Anymore." She dropped trou. A gore-streaked appendage hung from between her legs, something masquerading as a phallus in lieu of taking care of what was beneath it all.

Process of Elimination

"The only caveat here is that I'm not gonna tell you what her name is. You'll know who it is once you see her face, but you can't let that stop you if I'm paying you a hundred grand."

"I don't even know *your* real name, Fader. We're all just numbers working with numbers here," said #1.

He already fucked up. While talking deets with Fader, he couldn't help looking up who lived at that address.

Oh shit, he thought.

Aria Connolly.

"Ah, only thing is I'll need it all up front," said #1.

"Whatever. Anything to keep my wife and kids safe."

Once #1 got the cash and her gate code from Fader, he lost his nerve.

Aria Connolly was the former heiress to Connolly Clubs, an upscale chain of Florida golf courses. That bridge was scorched after a prison stint for extorting the family estate. Two security guards also had their throats slit, though there wasn't evidence to pin *that* on her. But everyone knew she did it, her OJ-style glaring arrogance dripped into a smirk off the far side of her lips.

Upon release, she was back on her bullshit – her first victim, Fader. As his mistress, she coerced access to his millions. When confronted, she vowed to kill him, his wife and children if he left her.

Fader believed it.

So did #1 – the way a wealthy ex-hitman like Fader was stuttering, it made him shudder to do the job, more so now that he could put a name with the fear.

"I think I know another guy..." he thought.

"Yeah, simple elimination, though I can't tell you

who. You're better off not knowing. But you'll get $75,000. Here's the address."

#2 agreed. #1 dropped off the money and the gate code. Then #2 did a google search with the address.

"Fuck, that chick who was all over the news five years ago? I ain't doing this..."

It unfolded in slight variants: the *bucks* were passed along with Aria's gate code and address. Whackers 1–5 skimmed off the top – the price of doing business with the hot potato anguish of harboring Aria's identity.

"Here's the residence – don't look up the resident. Just do it..."

Hushed like an echo through the outskirts of the everglades.

But #5 knew the perfect guy. All these contract killers were too smart to take the job. #6 was a guy dumb enough, just in simpleton love with wacking people as if they were flowers he was kicking off someone's lawn. By the time it got to him, the price on Aria's head was a clinking coin in a tip jar.

But he went for it.

Gate code entered.

Car parked.

Steps ascended.

Ear to the door.

All Aria needed to see was a crouching silhouette through the fibers of her window curtain.

All #6 knew is that he needed both hands to stop the blood cascading from his neck. Gasping, he saw his .38 tumbling down the stairs.

"What am I worth?" she asked, commandeering his weapon.

"10,000!"

This is like death for a former heiress to hear. She didn't believe it. She coerced #6 tell her about #5 as she learned his $10,000 was in his car.

She grabbed the cash, telling him to GTFO.

Now it's an inverted pyramid scheme. Aria, the bottom point traveling up and wide to collect her worth. #5 spilled it to #4, these grizzled killers now mere kindling for her wildfire ascending this capsized mountain of cowardice.

"What am I worth?" she asked each one.

"Forty-grand!" said #4.

"Fifty-grand!" said #3

"Fucking seventy-five grand, I'm sorry!" said #2.

Gushing with adrenaline at each mounting number on her head, her esteem satiating at this twisted auction of human value.

"A hundred grand, please just take it and leave me alone!" said #1, backing up as he left his skim on the floor.

She didn't need #1 to tell her where #0 lived. She hightailed it to wipe him out in more ways than she could count.

It was 1:30am when Aria stood outside Fader's gated property. Her eyes welled up, thinking of her dead father who cut her off. She pondered Fader's kids. She looked at her car containing all $100,000 – her prize for survival.

She turned and walked back to her vehicle.

"I think I know another guy..."

Closed for Take-Out

"Don't watch the news, don't go on the computer," I kept telling myself. I saw the pattern in the way it exacerbated my brimming anxiety. The death toll was mounting, and as the virus mutated and multiplied, so did the ever-changing protocol.

"Just sit home and watch TV – it's easy!" I heard them recommend. For the first time in history, it appeared both the powers that be and a large swath of the population finally got what they always wanted: Couch-lock. But what a time to be living, when staying informed was repellant to one's stable mental health. The last time I broke down and turned that damned thing on, I was informed by their latest contrarian punchline, where some reporter was claiming that stress made you more susceptible to the contagion.

You really couldn't win.

It was enough to make anyone fucking lose it. Especially when you considered the first instinct of The Great Unwashed. These assholes just wanted to cover their own butts, buying toilet paper by the truckloads, hoarding it – even bragging about it cruelly.

I swear I didn't see that one coming.

What I needed was something that might actually see these assholes coming from a mile away, then put a stop to them before they get any closer – residents looting their own neighborhoods might be their next logical degeneration.

I was going to buy a gun.

I was gonna get in on the ground floor of this doomsday's worst-case scenario.

I live in an unincorporated town thirty miles outside of Phoenix, with no more than two functioning businesses –

one bar and one gas station. Besides that, we're all tarp roofs on dirt roads. Long story short, we have to go up the hill to get any real supplies. I had already fought the crowds at Wal-Mart up there yesterday, filling my cart full of non-perishables for the alleged long-haul of the lockdown.

I brought back more than food. I returned home with such a rejuvenated misanthropy that I shut the blinds, locked the doors. My only happy thought was now being enforced by the state – don't go out again unless it was an absolute emergency.

But survival is an emergency, and I was simply planning ahead.

Tommy, get your gun.

Turns out I wasn't the only one with a killer survival instinct. I pulled up to Independence Guns and Ammo, cursing out loud as I saw a line going all the way around the block, as if it was a fucking nightclub. As I gawked, a car cut me off from the last parking space I was obviously aiming for.

"This is turning into a goddamn race," I thought.

I parked on the street and sprinted into the last place in line. I stood there with nowhere to put my accumulated panic besides my anxious, tapping feet. I peeked around the corner to get a better look at the pace of the line, to see if these people were keeping it moving or turning into social hour.

The chatter claimed the latter.

"Hey, Tom! You too, huh?" The timing was uncanny for my next-door neighbor Riley to notice me. Didn't know him real good, we mostly just waved when we checked our mail at the same time. So even though were five miles away from our houses – this was, I guess, much more intimate.

"Hey, Riley. Uh, yeah, I guess so!" It was the best I could do, because I was cut off by my other neighbors, Vicky and George, who recognized my voice.

"Ha! Heya there, Tom! Fancy seeing you here," said George.

"Yeah, where's *your* date?" added Vicky. "Me and George are making this a little date!"

"Heh, yeah, I can see that," I said, "You two are, uh... just great." I lied through my yellow teeth trying to hide the fact I was furious they were all ahead of me in line.

Then, another guy from my road waved to me. Then, that teenager that's always tearing up the road with his dirt bike – guess he's eighteen now and he finally feels friendly enough to wave, after all these years? *Was my whole neighborhood here?* I thought, as the line finally picked up speed.

It really did seem like my whole neighborhood when I saw the Mitchells walk out, huddled together though clearly more sullen than the rest of these grinning psychos. The Mitchells were an old married couple, late into their eighties. The nicest two people on our road, if I had to pick with, you know, a gun to my head. I had more rapport with them than anyone, as they exuded an old-school pleasantness that wasn't complicated – exactly what you wanted in a low-maintenance neighbor. Besides, their longevity as a couple gave me hope, in a world that no longer seemed to support that kind of bond, enduring or not.

So, I waved. I waved harder than I've ever waved to anyone. I know they saw me, because they seemed to grow even more solemn as they tried not to look at me a second time.

But they wouldn't wave back. Everyone saw the snub. I felt like the dumbest guy on Earth, now just as overeager as the rest of them.

"Someone must be having a bad day!" someone callously cat called.

Right when my gut told me I should check on them

when I got home, the line surged, interrupting my thoughts of goodwill. It appeared they were letting maybe five people in at a time. I was second in line out of the next five.

Minutes passed. A rotund guy wearing an Independence Guns and Ammo T-shirt came out and started counting people, a dreadful look on his face. He went back inside, re-emerging thirty seconds later.

"Folks, I regret to report we are actually out of guns! I repeat, we are out of all firearms for today and the rest of the week but would be glad to take your info if you'd care to backorder a firearm of your choice today..."

An ugly sound emanated from the line behind me, the hissing serpent wrapping around the building. A deflation of disappointment, panic, and rage, as if it this guy was robbing them of their freedom. I bailed, frustrated and sick, obsessing how bad I wanted one simple .45. But I refused to be part of this coiling skid-mark of humanity any longer.

I drove home, bringing home nothing other than the grim thought that I may now be the only house on my street without a gun.

I surveyed the passing commerce. Every restaurant, bar and coffee shops now with signs OPEN FOR TAKE-OUT ONLY. This was getting serious. Considering our area was economically compromised before the pandemic hit the fan, it was doubtful some of these businesses would recover from the new 'no-gathering' law.

Maybe they should all start selling guns? I thought, followed by a sorely needed laugh.

I pulled into my gravel driveway.

Right as I pulled the car into park, I heard a loud bang, immediately followed by another one.

I checked my tires only to realize it had all come from the Mitchells across the street.

I knew what that sound was, though I didn't want to admit it.

Guilt edging out fear, I acknowledged it was now mandatory I check in with them. I walked to the road, only to stop and stare at their house much too long for an emergency. I ran into my house. I grabbed the little ax I use for chopping wood, just in case. I had no idea what was going to be on the other side of their door.

Or else, I had really sharpened my denial skills since I last checked.

I stared at their house for a little while longer before I, the chicken, successfully crossed the road. Their shared 1999 Oldsmobile was in the driveway. I knocked on the screen door. It wiggled, barely closed. Once my eyes adjusted, I saw the wooden door was wide open like they were welcoming me.

But the Mitchells were both sprawled dead on their hardwood floor. Their heads lying in a pool of blood, eyes closed, mouths open. Their expressions still animated, as if they too, couldn't believe what they just did.

In my heart of scarred over hearts, I knew this was what I was going to find. Their uncharacteristic snub at the gun shop filled me with enough dread to think the worst, though I think it softened the shock when I saw it with my own eyes.

They each had a .45 in their hand.

The same kind I wanted to buy.

In Mr. Mitchell's other hand was a note. I touched his fingers, still warm, trying to find the guts to pry them open. When I forced them unclasped, I gave them a little squeeze since he'd never be able to touch anyone again, while I began reading:

We are sorry to whomever had to find us like this. It is nothing personal. We were very happy and simply didn't want to live out the winter of our years this way. The way things are now. So, we reserved one of our last fleeting rights — to go with God.

It was short, resolute, and bereft of malice or spite — just as you always hoped a double-suicide note could be. Though there was one part I may have read too much into — Hell, these days it seemed perfectly normal to search for your own hidden narrative in the deliberate — but that last line "to go with God" reminded me of the only reverent quip in Howard Beale's big speech in the film *Network* before he faints:

"Go with the truth — go with God! Go with yourself!"

These uncertain times called for that kind of divine rebellion. And in that strong gesture of certain permanence they knew they could never take back, the Mitchells were finished being buoys in a thrashing sea; exhibiting a near-extinct romantic integrity that our world may never see again.

And I concurred: Our world no longer deserved them.

I felt horrible, I really did. But I would have felt even worse if I didn't gently unclasp each of their hands from those .45s, liberating them from the tools of their painful exit.

I walked back across the road to my house, double fisting each pistol. I stuck them both in the air, in renewed vigilante triumph as I now felt caught up with the Jonses.

"My name is Tom Richardson and I am no longer open for take-out!" I said, perhaps louder than I should have. I closed the door, locking it behind me, then happily shut the blinds.

The Visitor

It was the Blood Moon. Suddenly, all the black girls were prefacing the transformation by calling me 'baby.' Every single one I encountered, as if they were finally initiating me into their secret order whose code had been convoluted; not only through centuries of their oppression, but a displaced guilt oozing out of my every pore. Now, the last drop purged – I was on their side. Now, they were all calling me baby – those *Angelitas Negras* – and I smiled.

Those once inaccessible angels had opened the gates to let the light in, shining down on what I truly desired, sculpted from my subconscious, free of guilt of whose heart would break as collateral damage, free of phantom social league limitations, free of my philosophies that were full of holes and meant to be broken anyway. Before, I was only allowed to dream of my perfect Bride of Frankenstein, where my every fetish, intricate sub-emotion, and twist of the eyes would re-animate her out of my humbled, longing vision.

But now, I am allowed.

You.

A paler shade in an eclipse of Mexican and German blood with a soft infernal dynamic that plumes you into smoke and honey. All the selfless empathy of a saint that still suffers zero fools like Kali. A figure of a belly dancer with an enveloping sunrise of an ass that seemed to be eating me sideways as I danced behind you, holding you tight at the nightclub. Relentless and unrepentant until the wee hours when we surrender behind closed doors and into each other's arms, lips locked, keyless. I feel you have actually been here all along.

This is what makes this moment difficult. You had

to go away for a while, much too soon.

But I found you. Over hills and strange towns, I followed my divining rod stirring beneath my belt as the thought of you touches me like a cool breeze, my manhood pointing the way. I find your room number. I find your room. I knock on the door. You ask, "Who is it?" through a knowing smile I cannot see but I know it's there. Much like you already know it is me behind the door, though many have come to visit you.

I have come to pay absolute tribute to you and I do not care about their rules.

I walk to the foot of your bed before climbing up, spreading my knees apart as I hover, advancing over you, planting my palms on each side of your head as my face slowly descends to yours. I trace your lips gently up and down with mine like a cat drinking a bowl of milk. I wait to hear you sigh before I dive my tongue into yours; they ooze and dart into one another like two small fishes fighting over bits of nourishment.

But I have passed one of my main destinations where I can show you rather than words cheating the sentiment. Slowly, I crawl backwards until my feet gently touch the ground, my torso now resting on the foot of the bed. I kiss your knees, giving them the weight of my head to direct them to either side, revealing your bare blossom I would have just admired for hours had I not just pressed my whole face into it. My tongue is possessed as it reacquaints itself with every ribbon and crevice of your gate. I cannot get close enough, until I decide I have redefined intimacy altogether. Yet my tongue cannot go any deeper – my face has taken full-residence, absolute foundation upon your mound. I'm afraid I might suffocate myself with desire until it occurs to me that there's plenty of equipment here meant to resuscitate me.

It's at that very moment that I tear off your hospital

gown.

You tear off my belt, ripping off my slacks like you're revving a lawnmower. I plunge into you as your whole body softens to welcome me.

It's midnight, well-passed visiting hours. But are we not paying good money to have you here? Are you and I not the only glimmer of hope in an institution that reeks of death, debt, and bedpans? Let us show it. I say we are both allowed. Let these hallways brim loud with your cooing as I reverse your pain. It is you who must stay in the hospital, yet it is you who are somehow keeping me alive.

Artificial Midnight

Jim could watch her sleep like this for the rest of his life. One look at Annette in peaceful surrender was a viewing into the absolute. There was no looking away.

"*Amazing*," he thought, "*How someone sleeping so soundly can keep me awake like this…*"

Beautiful and yet resigned was Annette. His drowsy musings continued within his head as he smiled, "*Sleep is perfection – when you are pretty, and you don't even know it. There is no more exalted potentate!*"

He was a heavy smoker, always with a lighter handy. There was no night-light, so Jim held up his Zippo far enough from her face to not wake her with its heat, but close enough to pronounce her rounded features, illuminating every cute freckle, to fully enjoy this elastic moment, stretching… It pained him that he had to keep it away from her eyes, his favorite glow of hers.

The silence had been so present, so enveloping, yet a shrinking umbilical cord, a candle burning from both ends, fusing the two of them together. Jim noticed a weight to his breathing, threatening to soil the pristine moment. He imagined what this might look like to someone who might open the door. He was beginning to creep *himself* out – though he stood by the sincerity of his pining. He flicked the cover back over the Zippo with a soft snap and slid it back in the right- hand pocket of his Levi's. Since he was lying down, he stuck his whole hand in the pocket to make sure it made it in there securely. When his fingers hit the bottom of the lining, he felt something else. He immediately tried to tell himself that what he was clearly touching wasn't what he was clearly touching.

The fucking key.

"The fucking key" he gasped. "Fuck!" he screamed as he squirmed. "Oh fuck!" he said, attempting to cover a shadow of tears.

He knew he fucked up, but still checked his small, riveted Levi pocket in attempt to further delude himself.

Nope. Nothing there. Just the wrong one in the big pocket. He felt its rounded head to confirm the worst – what he had was the key to his safe at home. He had clumsily given Miguel and Danny the key to his P.O. Box, the one that had the rectangle head.

"Fuck!" he screamed.

She began to stir. Her head shifted slightly. *Impossible.* Impossible against the plan, which was slowly unraveling. He wanted to lull her back to sleep by rubbing her shoulders but was afraid to touch her, afraid to do anything now except fucking panic which only required fear.

Annette's arm raised up to wipe the drool from her mouth. "Thirsty," she whispered. "God, I'm fucking thirsty." She had been asleep for three hours, which is when she usually got up to get a drink of water, her sleep cycle rock solid.

Jim stared at her, shaking, watching the inevitable unfold. She'd figure it out any second. There wasn't a damn thing he could do.

She swirled to half-life, molasses-paced, handicapped by what Jim dissolved into her citrus that apparently wasn't enough to take her to the near bottom of oblivion. She propped herself on her right elbow, lifting herself up.

Her head whacked the wood.

"Ow! What the fuck?" she screeched as she dropped down, holding her head. She tried to rise again, with greater force but same result. Unyielding.

She threw her fist to the side, only to hit more solid

maple.

"Jim? Jiiiiiiiiiiim!" Her hands scurried until they found him to her left. She began scratching at him. "Where the fuck are we? What the fuck is this?"

Jim gave his private consternations a rest, though he couldn't stop wheezing his words.

"I'm... I'm so sorry. I wasn't going to go through life without you..."

"Jim!!" she scream-cried. "Jihihiiiiiim!" She knew. She began to kick the roof of the coffin as she continued to batter her husband with whom she had been initializing divorce proceedings all week.

Needless to mention, he had been uncooperative.

"... and this is the only way I knew how. I wanted to suspend us in certain amber. Stay beautiful. You don't know what you were doing by wanting to leave."

He continued as reality began to suffocate her, his voice growing wheezier by the sentence.

"You always told me 'show don't tell.' I married you and even *that* wasn't even enough, Annette! What is more commitment to you? How do you define it? We signed a contract with our hearts! Death do us part!"

She was a flurry of fists, legs, deafening screams pummeling Jim in their wooden finality, now thwarted three-fold. If Annette didn't desperately claw him to death, the boys would surely get to him once they realized his fatal blunder.

Jim was going to die – just not the way he wanted to.

***

Concurrently, six and change above freshly compacted earth, Miguel and Danny both wielded rusty shovels they would later throw away, patting down the final layer of dirt on their

$500,000 contract, paid by a man who would be both murderer and victim.

His way.

Miguel squinted, swearing he heard something muffled from the depths of their dirt mound.

"Did you hear that? I fucking thought I heard..." Danny asked, screwing his face up.

"Nope! Didn't hear anything." Miguel replied bluntly.

"No? Me neither then..." Danny concurred with a knowing nod.

The sun was beginning to blast them relentlessly, typical for noon in the mid-desert. This spot was chosen for its proper, workable soil, due to the moisture of winter's mountain snowmelt collecting in this unique basin that was greener than one might expect for such an arid climate. If they went to the proper high desert, or lower, they would be working with the constant spill of sand. It had to be done fast as inhumanly possible, with one stop before they would disappear to Mexicali.

Danny saw his sweat dropping onto the fresh dirt as he put the finishing pats on the mound. "All right, that's quitting time," he half whispered. "Let's go to Phase Three and get paid."

Miguel sprinkled the remaining contents of the bag of Bermuda seeds on the spot. Danny threw his shovel in the back of their wagon pickup, followed by Lazlo's, which he tossed in with a careless racket.

"What the fuck man, you trying to send echoes through this valley, get us fucking caught?" Danny scolded.

"My bad," Miguel admitted. "Let's just get going..."

The next stop was Jim's house, left unlocked, tucked into the crevices of the north side hills that surrounded the valley. Jim had Miguel and Danny over the night before while

Annette was at work, showing them where he kept the safe containing their pay. He had opened it for them, proving the cash was all there, and let them count it all themselves; they agreed they wouldn't be allowed take it until the job was done.

Jim used a key lock on the safe. He knew that his wet-brained memory was too much a liability to remember a combination, especially while his life was narrowing down into sweet oblivion with his wife, forever, just as they agreed upon their wedding day.

They simply fell in love too quick. They married only nine months into meeting. Hell, they were well into their 40s and didn't want to miss a chance on true love. Jim in particular, was done pussyfooting.

But perhaps they should have gotten to know each other first.

***

Annette harbored a lifetime of unchecked childhood trauma, which grew into a runaway train of rage issues – she was beginning to see an abuser form within herself. Jim was a rich kid who had hobnobbed his way into the art world, posing as the sensitive artist type without actually producing any work. Instead, he threw conceptual art warehouse parties – his talent lay in acquiring his parasitic commissions, building a magnetic and monopolizing name for himself. Inadvertently he constructed an attractive ruse of *struggle* while possessing the tell-tale sign of spoilage, his peers and loved ones constantly lavishing him with praise. When he didn't get that cloying acclaim, he headed straight back to the bottle, tempting fate with his chemically-padded tug-of-war; the intertwining worms of fatalism and addiction constructed the rope which bound him. After nearly a year of bats-into-Hell domestic dystopia with Annette – whom he had vowed to be with forever – that rope finally snapped when she threatened to leave.

He sacrificed a lifetime – his perpetual public eye L.A. spotlight – when he bought them that house in the country. In his shattered mind, there was nothing left to give up besides his own bursting trust-fund, to assure they stayed together, to preserve their fleeting youth; not in amber... but inside a large, opulent casket, made from the wood from which it seeps.

Jim dug his own hole. The night before the lowering ("it's not killing, they kept saying – just *lowering*!") after the money was revealed in the safe, he took Miguel and Danny to the spot where he had painstakingly uprooted earth for the burial. It was well off trail, on the other side of the highway, a sentimental vista where he and Annette had watched the sun come up on their long first night in the country. After the simple procedure was discussed, the three dispersed. Jim rushed home to knock out, trying not to think about the next day.

There was no turning back with Miguel and Danny. Each had a sizable gang-related body count under their belts, and Jim knew damn well that they wouldn't hesitate to kill him *their way* if anything went wrong. Annette would come home from her bartending gig around 2:30am, in theory, go right to bed, so Jim could wake up and have a specific breakfast waiting for her, to lead to a perfect last morning together, before the Midazolam in their tangerine juice took its intended coma-inducing effect.

He saw her head struggling against its own weight. He led her to their bed, where they both surrendered to their in-tandem abyss at 9:30am.

Miguel and Danny were instructed to wait till 11:00, to ensure the couple were well on their way to their still-pulsing void. They slowed down on their street to make sure no one was standing or sitting inside. They backed in, ass up to their unlocked front door. A basic sequence: turn the knob, walk inside, head to the bedroom to make sure they were properly zombified, head to the shed, pick up casket, place by bed, pick her up first, place her inside, then him, close the lid, pick up casket, carry through living room, *sliiiiiiide* into the back of the truck, and Phase One was complete.

Now, Phase Two. It looked like someone tried to pave Jim and Annette's road twenty years ago. But that amateur job would not weather the hard monsoons and crackling heat of the desert, leaving once passable asphalt as nothing but erratic, jagged islands of cement on top of uneven, craggy earth. No choice but to to drive one mile an hour in nonsensical zigzags to avoid biting their own tongues off, still tempting risk of waking them. It was nature vs. civilization vs. two stranger's unknown metabolism to drugs vs. cold hard cash.

"Just imagine it's a bomb in the back." Danny kept telling Miguel from the passenger's seat, reassuring him by osmosis of terror. "Easy, easy... Feather that break. Don't even barely press the gas, bro. Just keep light, swerve easy through that shit... You got this," he whispered, teetering on a breathy threat.

There was the highway. They whispered *hallelujah*.

Now they just had to cross halfway across the 62, get into the turn lane, flip a bitch and make their first right down a more civilized, smoothly paved street, then to the old forgotten service road. Done. *Smooth dreams from here, homie.*

Before they turned onto the dirt road, Miguel leaned out the window and looked down at the mouth of their impending path.

"Aw, we're gooood..."

He saw a trail of the same three pairs of sneaker prints, still intact from the night before, which meant no one had been down the road since. Their tire tracks would help erase them further, as they had made sure to walk on opposite sides of the road last night, five feet equidistant.

They recognized the large rock to the left, where they knew to veer left off-road, about a half mile or so down a scabrous but even pass, into one of those long crevices the creeping noon sun will make dark shadows out of, like demon claws tightening on the range.

There it was. Jim had dug a long ramp into the ground, leading to the bottom of the conscious grave. Miguel slowly pulled around a half-circle so the back was facing the job, turning the car keys towards him. They acted quickly yet gingerly, exiting the vehicle as they ran to the back of the truck as if the ground was pure glowing magma. Diligent and solemn as two *bona fide* pallbearers, they pulled the casket out, each grabbing an end. Their biceps bulged in quivers, their teeth clenched, foreheads perspiring into their eyes as they scooted their sneaks backwards to the dirt ramp. They laid it down – laid *them* down – but not once today had they personified the weight of the object.

"Eyes on the prize. Don't think about what you're actually doing, man..."

Danny ran back to the cab to grab the rope and hook. He ran to the casket, attached the hook to the handle, and led the slack back to Miguel, who was standing at the other side. He got behind, picking up the rest of the slack behind him, as they both began their own tug of war with time vs. mortality vs. commerce.

Their teeth unclenched, caught off guard by how easy their effort was. It was sliding right down, as if it were meant to be. A little nervy then, as they saw the front of it lift up as the back of it made it to the bottom, *but that's just from the angle we're at, man…* Danny gave Miguel the rest of his slack as they calmly let it go level.

No stone unturned – Danny ran down the decline to grab the hook off the handle, coiling up the rope. He put his left ear to the coffin. *Beautiful silence* he mouthed up to Miguel, making a circle with his thumb and index. Miguel took that as a cue to throw the first shovel-full of dirt on Danny, reducing him to an image of a chimney sweep. He ran up the incline to tackle him before coming to his senses not to engage in horseplay. Instead, he grabbed the other shovel, digging it into the moist pile of earth, jamming it down there with renewed, focused adrenaline.

They fell into rhythm like a seasoned chain gang, like they had done this a million times, though considering their accumulated fatalities, this was the strangest one. What happened to the tried-and-true assassinations they were known for? *Fucking psycho* they kept saying under their breath, for once not referring to themselves.

Twenty minutes later, they were patting the last of the dirt on the mound.

"Did you hear that? I fucking thought I heard…" Danny asked, screwing his face up.

"Nope! Didn't hear anything." Miguel replied bluntly.

"No? Me neither then…" Danny concurred with a knowing nod.

Six feet below, a struggle was underway. The blunder was out in the open, inside their claustrophobic quarters, along with Jim's stuttering attempts to explain his romantic certitude. Jim's Zippo was now extinguished, the interior an indistinguishable black. Annette pummeled Jim sideways, though her arms tired quickly while she realized the oxygen was depleting.

To conserve energy, she switched to her legs,

squashing Jim with all her might into his side of the casket, hoping the pressure would puncture his lungs.

Her way.

All Jim could do was scream and cry *sorry*, but there were no give backs.

He had committed.

Doubled down.

Coupled up.

He prayed she would stop so he could break the really, *really* bad news, that the boys would be back to kill them whether or not they were able to withstand their last gasps.

***

Miguel shook his head and whispered *fucking psychos* for the tenth time that day. He drove down the highway with more confidence than before, but what they just did was coming down hard on his conscience – a reflection he knew not what to do with. It was more twisted and illogical than their most unjustified retributions, where they had killed for the sake of killing, to communicate to rival gangs that they were on top of the pecking order and to be feared. But this was fucking with his head. He was *getting* the fear.

"Fucking *psychos*..."

"Quit fucking saying that, bro!" Danny scolded. "Stop fucking thinking about it..."

They pulled up the back driveway to Jim and Annette's to finish off phase three. They pulled up, exited the truck, then went to the back bedroom patio where the safe was. They opened the sliding glass door and entered the now vacant abode.

The men kneeled at the safe, breathing heavy, knowing they were nearly at the finish line. Miguel went to his key ring for the tiny key and surgically entered the keyhole, fingers shaking.

Rejected.

He struggled a bit. He struggled more. The key went in but wouldn't turn. He yanked it out, examined the teeth, then stuck it back in. The sequence of teeth wasn't sliding in smooth like it should have. Miguel's heart began to anger-race.

He whispered. *"Motherfucker..."*

"Don't fucking tell me, bro..."

"I will fucking tell you, bro! He gave us the wrong fucking key!" Miguel snapped. He picked up the safe and threw it against their closet mirror, shattering it as he instantly regretted the racket.

"Fuuuck! Fuck, bro!"

"What do we do?"

"Get in the car, just get in the fucking car..."

Miguel felt faint buzzing with blind rage, his adrenaline rocking him back and forth in the driver's seat. Danny punched his side of the door, mumbling Spanglish obscenities as they peeled out, conspicuous, all their stealth intentions flying out the window behind them.

Now with nothing to lose but a lesson to give, they arrived back at the site. They parked, bee-lined to the back of the truck, grabbing the shovels without a word. Danny was the first to throw his shovel into the mound, as they began to re-perform Phase Two *in reverse...*

The fresh soil slid buttery through their tools as they jammed 'em in with ease, back in the previous hours' rhythm but faster, faster... Grunting with bloodlust vs. time vs. vigilante justice.

Miguel paused, dripping sweat.

"Hey! When we get it open... Like this..."

He took the shovel to his neck to pantomime the

couple's elimination. *Their way*. They finally felt themselves again, in control of a vengeful assassination of someone who had done them dirty.

The struggle down below proceeded with no caution. Nothing left to lose for Annette, who was making Jim gurgle with her heels against his stomach, crushing him into the once-cradling sarcophagus. Jim cried, trying to explain the more artistic, romantic elements of his desperate, mortal stunt. How he ran out of bullshit, ran out of patience, ran out of future, ran out of logic, but his timing was off as they were both running out of air.

He never could read a room.

Gasping for their lives, Annette manipulated the Reaper's clock, expelling her rage while Jim spun the roulette wheel of what words he could randomly conjure to make them die in peace, all the while knowing that the gavel was pounding down, shovel-full by shovel-full.

He could hear them.

Gaining ground by displacing ground.

He told her what was coming. He apologized profusely. He had done all he could.

He committed.

He should have *been* committed.

A strange peace came over him as Annette eased off her heels, her pressure ceasing. But it was only in order to change gears slightly, as she merely returned her hands to his throat, applying all strength she had left, squeezing the guilt out of his larynx. Jim resigned to die, to atone for his last sin. *Everyone else's way*. He had but one final request.

"All I wanna do is see the sun! One last time! Let me see the sun, Annette!"

The slick swishes of the men's stabs into earth were jolted with a *thunk!* The shovel strikes accelerated to jackhammer pace as they struggled to find the four corners, possessed as they scrapped the thinning layer of dirt off the varnished surface, quickly shining through the moist earth. They could hear Jim's voice screaming with anguish. It excited them, they knew he was alive, so they could finally end this job. *Their way.*

Miguel shoved his hand halfway into the dirt and the casket door to get a grip. He swung it open. Annette screamed with displaced embarrassment. Busted. She pulled her thumbs away from where Jim's eyes once were, now bloody pulps of dripping gore spider-webbing his jowls.

The couple wheezed a deep-end death-defying breath, as Jim did the only thing he could to prove his skewed innocence. Trembling, he lifted his arm over him, like the big hand on the twelve to pray God start from scratch, holding the safe key over his head in arcane surrender the men couldn't understand.

The All-The-Way House

The room assumed me.

The only way to return to the All-the-Way House was from the top floor. The third story. Though a dread fills my mind that there may be an attic as well.

I'm not going to lie – I know the attic is there. I knew the whole time. But you don't ever, *ever* enter the attic – not through its window from the outside or the floor hatch from the ceiling of the third floor. We are better off just forgetting about it, like the fourth story of the Congress Hotel in Tuscon where they burnt out John Dillinger's gang after that big fatal shootout. They're probably all still up there, their foreverbones. But it belongs to no one, nothing but an unspeakable denial now, and not even those splintering stairs can sustain our curiosity.

It's none of our business, whatever happened up there.

But I've misled us already.

There I was, on the third floor of the big house, in the room you had to walk through in order to get to all the other bedrooms. As if its architect designed it specifically for voyeurism, the object bereft of privacy, as we knew someone would have to end up living in there.

We *all* lived in there. The room was squared off, framed by two squishy, spineless L-shaped couches, their color dark but indiscriminate with tell-tale large stains, like whole continents before they began to split and drift apart. The couches flush against walls painted sky blue, so it appeared you were free-falling – that is, during that one hour of mid-afternoon when the sun was placed just so, that it was able to ricochet and penetrate the cracks of endless hallways through the jambs of closed doors. There were no windows in the blue room, so you never knew what time of day or night was since, the room's dimmer seemed to be stuck on the faintest setting. Was it beyond repair, or did the dimness make it easier to get away with living this way, where you couldn't quite focus on anything or notice the rising tides of neglect?

We'll never learn.

Though I have no memory of being outside, my daytime vision began to come into focus with this strained lighting.

I see her.

Ensconced in the angle of the sofa, her denim legs tucked under her. Her hair is an unkempt short black bob, her general essence boasting a tomboyish quality in a thin black T-shirt with gauzy holes, possibly moth-eaten. I am instantly in love with her relaxed, approachable disposition until I realize she is staring right at me, in paralytic judgment.

We share an eternity of a moment, locking eyes.

Mine: Curious and willing to surrender.

Hers: Disappointed, wishing she could change me already.

She speaks.

"So, where have *you* been?" she asks, already with a condescending tone that lets me know that no answer I give would suffice.

"Well, I've been out there, trying to do some good?" I was so nervous that I answered her question with another question, to show her I was immediately willing to change my response. I pointed to *out there*, at the periwinkle wall.

"Yeah, well that's hilarious," she said, shaking her

head. "Why do you always think you're better than all of us?"

Suddenly, I realize the blue room is full of others, taking up every inch of both sofas. It's everyone I have ever known, cuddling somehow apathetically, aggregated from their counterpart as an archetype's spokesperson. But they, also, are too disinterested to speak, each somehow able to glare at me with their heads downcast. They too, disappointed I am no longer one of them, therefore I am not to be trusted. Some of them smirk, shaking their heads in pity towards me, before turning to the girl as if to say, "Why are we wasting our time?"

And with that, they have disappeared again. Not a vaporous poof nor a mystified fade, just no longer there, leaving the girl to continue mind-fucking me in grating slow-strokes, where everything I do or say is the wrong thing to keep her,

or I,

or this story,

further from climax.

Frustration achieved the best of her.

"See? You made them all leave again! They all went back to their rooms! They're too sad to even hang out now! You know how bad it gets when they're alone! You better hope they don't see you again on your way out."

"You... don't remember how to even get out of here, do you?"

Before I can respond, she reassures me:

"Well, you can't go upstairs, cause, well... we don't even *talk* about upstairs. You can't go out *that* door, 'cause that will just lead to all our bedrooms and now if anyone sees you, you're going to pray to God you could just turn back time. I can already hear you scream, 'if only I never left the blue room!' And you have to pass their bedrooms to get downstairs, but you can't get downstairs 'cause some of them are in the kitchen. Everyone always ends up in the kitchen, crowded up as if there's nowhere else in this fucking big house to go! But they think that just cause that's where the booze is, that something will eventually happen there. But nothing ever really fucking happens there!" she said, shaking her head in disbelief of her own words, our own lives.

"Okay, well... what if I..."

"Oh, fuck you! You wanna get down to the basement, don't you? You know that room has been flooded for years, right? You can't. Even. Touch. The bottom! I mean, be my guest, but you're not going get to the bottom of anything! You want to be some kind of hero, don't you? Is that what this is all about, you showing up here again when we were just getting used to you being gone?"

I didn't want to go to the basement until the moment she forbade me to, before she turned it into a backhanded dare. Suddenly it was all I wanted – a cold-seeking lust, a magnetic pull into the dark waters she promised. In my mind's eye I could see the black mold forming on its shitty stucco ceiling, stinking murk perspiring onto the walls then dripping into the opaque soup again. I wanted to dive into the bottomless, dissolve with it, acquire secrets I would never be able to share with anyone because there was a good chance I would no longer be alive.

I didn't say another word. I just stared right at her. I noticed a sound – not one I heard, but a sound I *felt*. A droning static of obscene dog-whistle frequency that would render words meaningless anyway, her and I both paralyzed by each other's fixation, a contest of intimate endurance that our pores slowly suffocated from.

Suddenly, a moment of apparent mercy:

"Okay, listen... There's one way out of here. Right there."

She pointed to the fuse box.

"You were always too much of a coward to deal with the blackouts we had when it would storm, otherwise you would have known what was really on the inside of there. Go ahead, look!"

`The hinged-shut fuse box was the size of a wall calendar. I walked over, my mind muzzled by trepidation, unable to trust such an erratic 180 in her mood, fearing it could be another trap of faith and limit, of desire and denial. I unhooked the latch, cautiously pulling it open. It revealed a window to the residential night. I peered closer to focus on the view of the whole world with its lights off, not even a single porch bulb to welcome anyone home. A suburban abyss, a world evacuated. I looked down at the backyard – once a driveway, now overgrown with weeds as tall as adulthood, swaying with no spine in the sad, struggling wind trying to make anything move, to prove there was still life, a signal of how far things had gone. I saw a latch to open the screen-less glass, opened it slightly to make sure it worked, then looked back at her behind me.

"If this is a window, where's your electricity?" I asked.

"My electricity? Our electricity. Guess what? We never fucking had any!" she barked, leaning her head past her knees. "Just... a lot of chemicals, I guess."

Her unfounded scorn humbled to melancholy faster than I could process. She began to sob, staring right at me, attempting to trigger our paralysis again. I swung open the window and threw my arms around the pane, using all of my strength to pull myself up through a frame that seemed almost too small. But as I got my waist up and sat on it, my backside facing the strange freedom of a seemingly uninviting world, I realized it was made for me.

My hands grasping the windowpane's top exterior now, I looked down to the three-story drop. If I grabbed on to the bottom of the frame, and hung myself down, I knew it would be just under a two-level fall. This in mind, I forbade myself to look down as it might distract my adrenaline. Slowly I lowered to a hang as I heard her cries increase in volume, discord like a mist weaving through the blue room and out the window, trying to finally touch me, for once – her last-ditch effort when once we had all the time in the world.

I let go.

I landed in a forced squat, my ass nearly hitting the ground had it not been for some last-minute spring in my spine. I took a knee to lift myself up, but before I began the curious walk through the towering invasive grasses out the back gate, I turned around once again, towards the big craftsman house I had just escaped, all its residual ennui appearing to grab me by my collar. My head downcast with the weight of its negative radiation, I eyed the stairs that led from outside into the basement, half-exposed from the swamp murk, still slowly filling from years of oversight, delinquency, the utter fear of what they created. I looked through the small window, noticing couch cushions floating on the surface like lily pads, slightly turning and colliding then repelling, mimicking all the deceptive paths we chose through time.

I felt that pull to the bottom again, this time with confidence, knowing that I was going where only *they* were afraid to tread, therefore it was no longer off limits. I walked down the submerged stairs like a starlet's first baptismal entrance onto the screen, though finally rid of an audience, as this scene was mine and mine only with no eyes on the other side. Now, neck deep, I opened the paint-chipped door against the resistance of the elements, dunking my head under. As I felt the playful buoyancy lift my heels back to the surface, I opened my eyes to the richness of obscurity ahead of me. I began to wipe it all away to propel myself deeper, faster, each stroke more determined than the last.

Instead of reaching the bottom, I felt the fluid euphoria of the Neverdone pass through me, in defiance of neglect, and in perpetuity.

The Lonesome Defeat of Bridge Repair

He assumed that changing the locks on his house would have brought him a feeling of relief.

Safety.

Newfound independence.

Hell, the new doorknobs and key even boasted the brand name DEFIANT. But he was thrown off guard when the task proved more a shameful reminder of what he'd put up with for the last six months. A hangover of a different shade of dread, proving it was all open-ended, hard-boiled reality – not some nightmare he might soon wake from.

He put the key in the lock. It turned without complaint. He went inside. He'd broken it off with her in October. His therapist had told him to run. He ran, but into quicksand. It was now April – it had taken him a harrowing half-year to get her out of his house.

Embarrassment and exhaustion weighed heavily as he stood outside his front door, staring catatonic at the finished job of the lock change. He no longer had any fight left – she had drained him of his own survival instinct with her daily threats of suicide or, on a good day, an airtight manipulation of every conversation. It was the slipperiest of slopes. Every female he confided in seemed convinced that she was trying to push him to his most outer limits, so he might snap and strike her.

Then, *he* would be the bad guy.

He shuddered at the thought. He was far too terrified of her to even consider breaking his restraint, which itself had also entered the realm of the unreal. The fact remained – he now had to notify her that the locks had been replaced.

His ulcer churned. He didn't want it to be a surprise when she came to get the rest of her belongings; he was riddled with fear how she might react. He simply wanted to let her know beforehand so they could arrange a suitable time for her to come. Supervised.

A carefully worded email was sent, advising her of the lock change, ten minutes before she called him. Again. And again. Her name on his phone glowed with the shock of someone from his past he was trying to avoid for his own good. He writhed in bed until he finally picked it up on her sixth attempt.

"If you don't give me a key to get the rest of my things, I am going to smash every window! Or, if I'm in a good mood, I'll just break in! I know very well how to break into that house, you know…"

Dread snowballed into catatonia. He couldn't get a word in. His paralysis gave way to a narcotic numbness, though the antithesis of any kind of sought-after euphoria.

***

He panicked as he saw the clock the next morning. He hadn't willfully fallen asleep so much as his body and mind had simply shut down. Nocturnal discourse aside, he had forgotten to set his alarm and was now late for work. He showered, jumped back into the wrinkled clothes he had slept in. He grabbed his bag as he twisted the lock of the door behind him, shutting it with unnecessary force.

The keys chimed softly, still hung on the hook inside.

The second he heard it slam, he did the obscenity dance – stomping on the ground and whacking his right thigh, screaming under his breath. He refused to believe he had just locked his keys inside the house, but denial had recently got him nowhere. He was stranded.

Outside his own house.

Absurd.

He began casing the joint unsuccessfully, like a new lonely criminal with no apprenticeship, before finally giving up. It was her who had the skills to break in, not him.

As he began dialing her number, his skull seemed to shrink around his brain. His chest tightened. He exhaled heavily to release the pressure, a sigh that asked when the day would come when he would cease needing her.

Skattertown

Robbie flinched when he realized the time – five sharp. It was Happy Hour in what he and his three buddies called the Bro Abode, the multi-colored upscale condo in downtown Los Angeles where they lived like expired frat men.

Today, Happy Hour meant it was time for a special hour-long episode of *Skatterlife!* It was NOWTV's highest-rated amateur show that had quickly become a household name. This stand-alone episode was the most anticipated of the show's breakout year – the premiere of a new redux with a real news team, not just rogue cameramen who would upload their footage to the public domain site. This official pilot episode would recap the history of Skatter with proper narration and higher production values. The same team who manufactured the drug had recently bought the rights to the name and concept. You couldn't get any more *in-house*.

"Hey! It's on! *And it's on!*" said Robbie, hollering pseudo-tough to his condo-mates as he scrambled with the control to their NOWTV. They hastily placed their laptops down, hopping on the couch to join in full-screen bonding.

The opening shot: breath taking drone footage, silent as the techno-bird got a wide pan of downtown from the skyscrapers, before dropping to free-fall as if it had lost control. The footage swirled into disorienting blurs until it stopped mid-air with a perfectly framed shot – the vast savagery of L.A.'s new universal skid row. The canned sound of whipping wind and the new blood red block-letter logo spelled out SKATTERLIFE!, complete with an unnerving peanut gallery cat-call of the title.

"Yeeeah!" the bros approved as they settled in, transfixed as if it were the Super Bowl. But instead of opening cans of beer, the bros started busting out their respective stashes of Skatter: like popcorn that pops on your insides. Glass pipes were filled with the shard-like substance then passed around. Eyes bugging upon inhalation, euphoria immediate. The boy's anticipation for the show was insatiable – despite it already unfolding, well in progress. The beaming host and hostess, Mark Blameson and Maggie Hunter, looked exfoliated, powdered, ready to reflect and extrapolate on America's favorite drug.

"Hello America! I'm your host Mark Blameson...

"And I'm your co-host Maggie Hunter...

"...and we are here to introduce the re-boot premiere of SKATTERLIFE! The show dedicated to our country's wonder drug of choice: SKATTER! Now, we call it a wonder drug not because it's a cure all, but because of its wide-spread euphoria – a pre-occupation, a fascination, an all-inclusive *wonder,* if you will."

"Oh, you better believe I will, Mark!

As the camera panned to Maggie, she pulled a small glass pipe from one blazer pocket, a plastic baggie from the other. She filled the pipe with her own stash of Skatter without flinching, the matter-of-fact confidence of a pro.

"Hohoho, Maggie! You independent woman, you! Was that in the script? Either way, allow me..."

Mark leaned to his left, smiling congenially to light Maggie's pipe.

"Thanks, Mark! Such a gentleman."

Maggie drew in the vaporized contents. Her eyes dilated. As she withdrew the pipe, the camera closed-up on her face, focusing in on her red lips like a smoking fetish reel as she exhaled leisurely, slowly shaking her head left and right to make sexy zig-zag patterns of the exhaust. Slamming her hands on the desk, she white-knuckled the edges of wood as she scream-laughed, or laughed-screamed.

She offered a fresh bowl to her host as she dove into an erratic re-cap of the drug's comet trail. Since sitting in her seat was unimaginable, she signaled the cameras to follow her and Mark outside. They ran through the halls, skipping steps on every staircase down the old US Bank Tower from where they broadcast. The clunky, spaghetti-wired camera-crew trailed in hot pursuit, unsteady joy-toy footage beaming into all participating homes, until they landed street level, entering the sunset haze of a conflicted downtown Los Angeles.

"Oh damn!" Robbie screamed. "They're right there, like three blocks from us – so cool!"

The other bros joined in the escalation. They ran out to the balcony to see if they could spot Maggie, Mark and the bumbling crew. A perfect view of the US Bank Tower, they began waving as if they were drowning.

"Kevin, get back inside – let us know which direction they're headed!" Robbie ordered to his friend.

Down below the Bro Abode was just another street of downtown L.A. that had become a diseased tentacle of drug-addled Skid Row, now far reaching and integrated with a whole society hooked on Skatter. They lived on the same street as the US Bank building, yet were safely elevated, segregated from the savage throngs who couldn't afford the comedown.

"Looks like they're heading this way!" Kevin hollered back from the TV room. "But get back in here! Mark Blameson's talking again! Man, I feel like I could have a beer or a Skat with this guy. Do you think he would?"

Mark Blameson looked into the camera, his eyes wild and face slightly twitching.

"As the sun begins its reluctant descent onto downtown L.A., it casts a cold shadow on the concentration of this new vast, all-inclusive homeless swamp that from afar, looks like the massive crowd waiting eagerly for a concert to begin. But as you can see, there is no stage – only the unsure asphalt they limp across, looking for the men in red or blue."

Maggie interjected on cue, brimming with over-amplified displaced showbiz racism under the guise of talking "street."

"Yo! It's a sleepless 24/7 operation for the Bloods and Crips, fam! The boys in the red and blue now work together in indefinite truce for a common goal. They gotta be hellbent, yo! They gotta be keeping things moving or else downtown will become a stagnant heap of fly-infested carnage; which means they'd lose money, when means they'd lose their livelihoods, which means they'll lose their lives."

"It's kinda like we're *all* in the same gang now, right Maggie?"

"That's right, Mark! The gangsters aren't the real victims here – just entrepreneurs in a larger toxic cocktail with no end in sight. They sell Skatter: Crack on Steroids. The drug's namesake is taken from its glassy shard form, where the user can smoke it whole or crush and snort it with little to no trace of burn on the nostrils. A cousin three times removed from vintage Flakka, which took the ghettos of Florida for a nightmare ride back in 2014. But now in 2025, synthetic drugs have gone rogue. Skatter was created near-accident – its original manufacturers in China, always one step ahead of the DEA, changing the chemical make-up ever so slightly to stay legal while producing even more unpredictable effects. Now, with the massive popularity of Skatter, the Chinese have sourced their operations to its largest demographic – America – the largest production cell taking over the top floors of our old US Bank building in these congested bowels of downtown Los Angeles! Isn't that right, folks?"

Maggie looked back at rows of desperate faces now

crowded behind her, all cruel hybrid of grin and grimace. As the mob struggled to get in the shot, the crew jerked their cameras to and fro, tauntingly, struggling not to spotlight their missing arms and legs, nor the luckier ones replaced by robotic limbs. The faces in frame screamed for their fifteen seconds of fame.

"Oh, *now* we are having fun, right Maggie? Well, I don't wanna be a Davey Downer but to tell the whole story of Skatter, we've *got* to tell the whole story, right? We all know and love the high Skatter gives us to get us through the day of, well, eventually wanting more Skatter! But the most unique element of it − it can shoot you right through the roof. Now, excuse the poetry here, but the idea of Skatter is that you want to hit the roof, not go all the way through it − 'cause it can be scary out there!"

The camera panned to full-body shots of the crowd, now revealing the writhing, limping, handicapped masses screaming in dangling groans of agony or ecstasy, pointing to their synthetic limbs to either show off the shiny chrome or to protest their very existence. Mark takes pause to change gears, maniacally dipping into a condescending baritone of feigned-empathy, a popular go-to voicing for today's modern hack.

"You can call it an uncertain drug, or the perfect drug for our uncertain times. You see, no one could anticipate the rabid demand for Skatter, given the absolute horror it can induce. Skatter arrests the user into such an explosive high that it travels far past euphoria into an elevated yet paralyzing state, where the simulation of 'soul-death' takes hold. With the drug trapped in the user's system, a panic ensues after its pinnacle. The user then falls under a spell of the delusion that they must 'bleed' it out, hallucinating the essence of the drug as glass slivers under the skin, trying to escape through the pores. This often graduates from simple bloodletting to full dismemberment – as the user feels they are no longer human yet still trapped in a human body. With equal parts fear of soul-death and complete disregard to their mortal bodies, the user mutilates themselves until the corrupted high finally wears off, leaving them a different version of themselves than when they took the drug – indisputably!"

Mark points to a metallic leg attached to an otherwise able-bodied young white man, whose Elvis Costello glasses, beard, and faded, filthy LCD Soundsystem T-shirt suggest he may be what they once called a 'hipster' fallen on hard times, like most of his generation that couldn't afford the accompanying antidote.

"... Which brings us to what may be the most important, and sadly the most divisive element of Skatterlife: it's rather pricy counterpart, Gather. Once the Shatter high reaches its penultimate peak, the well-to-do user will apply Gather under their tongue for fast absorption and quick comedown. It's a white, flavorless paste that dissolves instantly in saliva. It takes the edge off the acceleration and subsequent delusions, making the user feel like their parachute just popped open mid-free fall. Now, the catch, Maggie?"

"Well, Mark, the catch is that Gather costs the user up to four times the amount of the street price of Skatter. For example..." Maggie grabs the hand of the nearest Blood for visual aid, conveniently to her to her right, as he was already dangling a shard-filled baggie for the camera.

"Sir, how much is that little baggie gonna run your customer, compared to... do you have a baggie of Gather so we can show the viewers?

"Ah, you know what m'am, we gotta keep that Gather under lock and key up at the penthouse of US Bank Tower, otherwise we gonna get straight robbed out here. But check it out – this baggie here of Skatter gonna cost the user next to nothin', five bucks for the high of your life and we never gotta inflate that. Now, that's thanks to Gather, which we sell now for the steady price of $100 a bag…

"Hold on, now wait a second here," Mark interrupted. "Now, the last time I bought Gather, earlier this week, it was only seventy-five bucks…"

"Inflation, homie. In order to keep the price set for Skatter, so everyone can get down with it, Gather gonna fluctuate a bit…"

"Fluctuate, meaning it'll go up and down?"

"To be honest, not exactly, brotha… We eventually going straight to the top with this stuff. Ask the big man up there." The Blood exuded ambition as he pointed to the top of the US Bank Tower.

"Oh no, we're not going there!" Maggie comically chimed. "I, personally, can afford my Gather, no problem. I'm happy with my product – I don't feel any nagging need to ask questions or rock the boat. That said, do you want to let our viewers know what else is offered from US Bank, besides our Skatter and Gather? In other words – how is a customer going to get a… well, what we'll call a 'quick tour' of another facility in there?"

"Sure, ma'am. See, this all may sound brutal, but the thing is, we take care of our customers. If someone's gonna get too high, and they can't afford the Gather, they gonna take it out on themselves… Hell, as you can see, right over there!"

The Blood pointed briskly to another satisfied, overindulgent customer. Leaning against a parking meter, he screamed in clenched teeth agony, nearly finishing the job of severing his forearm from his elbow, using a well-used rusty, crimson-streaked handsaw.

"S'cuse me, folks… Hey! Hey boys! Right there, go get him!" The camera shifted as Blood summoned his Red and Blue brigade to take care of the self-administered leper. In seconds flat, three men in sports jerseys – two in red, one in blue, show up to the user with a medical stretcher.

"Just two of you, he don't need all three! Hey Blue, come over here a sec!"

The Blood outstretched his arm to receive the Crip into the camera shot, as the same arm embraced his Blue homeboy, now brothers in arms.

"See, Skatter brings the world together. Everyone's included. We've been doing this truce for years now. Who gonna argue with this?" Blood asked in warped earnest. He and the Crip smiled for the camera.

"That's great! We are so glad the viewers at home get to see this kind of brotherhood. Imagine – no more war! Am I right, homies?" Maggie lifted her hand up to high-five the brothers as they boisterously obliged, smirking with slick confidence, if not low-key ridicule.

"Oh damn, okay, okay... we're getting carried away with all this love now," the Blood interjected. "So, where they takin' him, you asked? Robotics. That's level one. That fool is getting an upgrade, basically. We got the top docs, top techs working together over there. It's beyond artificial limbs, man. We got these metal arms and legs actually able to fuse with your major vessels where you be quarter 'bot, know what I'm saying? And it's turned into a bit of status symbol, right? Like people used to get grills in their mouths, gold chains and what not... You been in the game long enough, staying true, keepin' it real... not like these motherfuckers in the condos that can just afford the Gather willy nilly, that take all the danger out... When you see a cat in half-chrome coming toward you, you best stay on their good side and give respect!"

"Respect!" Mark Blameson mimicked, pointing to the camera, before high fiving a half-robot eager to get in frame. "See, viewers, what we have is respect down here at Skatter Ground Zero. As long as you can afford it all, no one is judging anyone…"

"That's right, and we are all here to help you get to that next level vibe!" said the Blood.

The caravan of media and street barnacles continued down 5th street, away from the tower. To the bros delight, the crowd was inching closer to the encroaching shadow of their condo.

"Dudes, they're coming this way!" Robbie hollered from the balcony to the others in the TV room. He took an overzealous hit from his pipe. "Hey! Right here!" he screamed to the mobile media blitz below a half a block away.

"We'll be right there!" Kevin called back to him, then whispered, "Let's get Robbie some Gather, I think he's getting to that point, yeah?"

The other guys agreed. Kevin grabbed the baggie of pricey counter-dope. They walked out to the terrace calm but wild-eyed, as Kevin grabbed him by the shoulder.

"Hey bro, open your mouth… you're getting crazy."

"Fuck you, bro! Damn right I'm getting crazy!" Robbie's optical vessels had since burst, giving him a demonic visual. "What are you guys even doing this for? You all wanna play it safe, bitch? I'm going down where it's all going *down*!"

Before Robbie's uptight compatriots could intervene, he had swung one leg onto the railing. He kicked himself off the edge into the oblivion of the swarming street level some four stories below.

"CAMERA ONE! TO YOUR LEFT!!!" said Mark, off-script, pointing to the commotion at the Bro Abode. A beautiful catch of real-time Skatter sensation, maybe the first of its kind – a jumper from the condos.

But they have everything, surely at least some Gather?
thought Mark and Maggie, their jaws dropping at the
silhouette of a man. It barely made sense, so for the premiere
episode of Skatterlife, it was *oh so perfect.* Mark and Maggie
imagined ratings soaring right out of the gates.

The crowd's gasps quickly ramped up to unnerving
eureka.

Like precision crosshairs, the camera lens got him
dead center, perfectly framed, following Robbie's dramatic
plummet to the asphalt. He appeared to be inviting his own
handicap, grabbing one ankle behind him, kicking the other
one in front like a parody of an antiquated skateboard trick.
He landed with a shuddering crack of splintered bone, a
scream of timeless anguish, his arms raised in arcane victory,
both middle fingers erect as if to say: forget the lazy privilege
of the Bro Abode.

Robbie was going straight to the tower.

Like clockwork, a Red and a Blue ran to his rescue
with their well-worn, bloodstained cot, a one-way ticket to
ultimate Skatter-Status of man-meets-metal.

"Well! I don't know if anything we see today is going
to top that, playa!" Blameson whipped his head directly into
the camera. "But what do *we* do when *we* come down, folks?"

"SKATTER!!!" the crowd screamed in unison with
Maggie as she looked back for approval, handing Mark a
fresh batch in their communal pipe.

"Now's the time where we like to interview the men
and women on the street, the common Skatterfiend who has
dedicated their lives – and limb – to keep Skatter alive!"
Maggie announced, as she pushed her way through the mob.

"And as we make our way through the good-natured
madness here, we like to find the most interesting person,
man or woman, who really stands out among the pack... Oh,
right there, what about her? Camera one, right over there.

Now, this gal looks great – she kinda has that punky, funky thing going on with her bad self!"

Sitting on the sidewalk Indian-style with a thousand-mile stare: a middle-aged black woman with frizzy dyed red hair, an army green trench coat over sludge-encrusted combat boots.

This was Sasha Darnell, a focused anomaly among the city's normalized turmoil. During her defiant yet adaptable meditations that could call anywhere a temple, Sasha's eyes would calmly open intermittently when outside invasive noise would intrude on her peace – the din radiating from the approaching media mob cutting through the full-volume from her earphones. She would play the only cassette she owned through a battered antique Walkman, the swirling transcendence of Alice Coltrane's *Journey in Satchidananda*. These ponderings of dissociation created an armor against the inescapable present. Sasha held no delusions of her firm place in the corruption – it was impossible not to acknowledge the cold steel of her left leg when the backs of her hands rested on her knees. She lifted her head reluctantly, her brown eyes gazing daggers toward the approaching mess.

"Well, hello soul sister number one!" said Blameson, shoving a mic into her grimacing face.

"You're on Skatterlife, live! Tell us, what are you doing to keep your love affair with Skatter on the up and up?"

Sasha glared silently at Mark and Maggie, the arrowheads of this block long spear popping her psychic survival bubble. Calmly, she pushed the mic out of her face, replacing it with her own middle-finger.

"Fuck you, bitch." she retorted, swiveling slightly to Maggie. "And fuck... you... too." She stood up, swinging her backpack over her shoulder as her coat fell to her legs. Both Sasha's arms raised up in defiance at the pathetic crowd attached.

"Fuck all you motherfuckers!"

Briskly she pivoted and walked away, a stride so confident it nearly silenced the catcalls. Still, the crowd stood dumbfounded why she wouldn't want to be on NOWTV.

"Looks like someone is having a bad day!" Maggie up-spoke, attempting to gloss over the contrarian nature of Sasha's exit out of frame. "Here's hoping she's on her way to cop some Skat!"

The depraved human cluster went nuts behind them.

Pride in their product.

It was no matter whether an onlooker deduced Sasha's psychobabble as mere random drug-addled delusion – she had places to go, people to see; and she wasn't even on her way to score more Skatter, despite her long 24 hours without it.

She had made a solemn swear to herself that she would get back into the Tower one day to carry out her vengeance on a man named Forrest Griffin.

Today was that day.

Every fiber of her body intuitively knew he was still up in that building, now, profiting off people like her.

There was only one high that could overshadow that of America's number one drug.

The jones of revenge.

That feeling was all the proof she needed that he was up there, somewhere.

Her arms swung with each step, propelling her stride towards the Tower, accelerating her speed. Sasha had seen that idiot jump from the condos – the brief but gory event prompted her sidewalk zone-out. The more she thought about it, the less the near-casualty disturbed her. It was more the condos that made her cringe – those ugly fucking condos. She talked out loud for company:

"...motherfuckin' gravestones of gentrification. Those ugly fucking condos, stacked in muted pastel like high-end building blocks for spoiled toddlers. Instant architectural parodies, calculatingly misplaced like houses of cards designed to fall. Goddamned playpens for the privileged, whose Mommy and Daddy send them money to afford their Gather for the comedown. But they never really come down... 'cept for least that one curious bitch that thinks he's one of us now. Shit..."

It was all revving her engine, her focus teetering. Though her brimming disgust for the new structures threatened to derail her path, she kept hoofing. Even when a heavy user wasn't on Skatter, their damaged physiology would often mimic its mood swings, prompting the user to find some more, just a little to level out, its cognitive dissonance igniting amnesia, next thing you know you're a rocket with nowhere to fly. Instead, the fuel fires out of every pore until you fall apart again under the atmosphere, melting down at lift off. Sasha told herself she wasn't going to do it again today, but there she was. The mere thought of it was its own green light to indulge. Besides, how else was she gonna get into that damn tower to have her show down with Griffin?

She had another point to prove to herself, that she would get in there without ODing again, or they'd take her other leg. Sasha knew she was tougher and smarter than that. She'd enter on her own terms. She needed her wits about her once she was inside, in case there had been any changes made to the layout upstairs. Then, if she found Griffin, she would need all the venom she could muster. She didn't need drugs, just one *good* leg.

"Okay, fine, I need drugs," she admitted as she prematurely reached for her machete from her back-sheath. *"Just not Skatter, so this won't count. This is merely practical,"* she thought as she reached into her backpack. She pulled out a bottle of Demerol and a hypo, half a bottle left over from

her first robo-leg surgery. The Tower sent you back on the streets with the thoughtful parting gift of vintage narcotics to ease the pain of metallic skin grafts.

She stuck the needle into the top of the bottle, plunged up the remaining contents, jammed it into the thigh of her leg, her flesh leg – which, to give credit where credit was due, had become inferior to her shiny, state-of-the-art robotic limb. She felt that cozy warmth of numbness spread over her haunch, quickly oozing down her leg right past her knee. She punched it for reassurance.

"Good enough," she said. Maturely now, she re-reached for her machete. Pre-maturely, she began to scream the most hellish howl she could erupt. Like a samurai as she swung the sword down on her thigh, slicing through skin, muscle, though not quite bone. Blood splashed through the blade. It rained onto the pavement, she screamed for her real-time pain, looking around for the Reds and Blues to take her away. She shrieked again as she brought the blade down harder on the same open wound, this time chipping the bone to marrow.

Besides the Demerol, her only anesthesia was the adrenaline of focused, salivating retribution.

She sheathed the machete, concealing it under her trench coat. It was going in the tower with her. She grabbed a butcher knife out of backpack as a decoy, wiping it on her pulsing gash to collect the deceptive evidence of blood.

"We got her!" she heard the Reds and Blues yell, scooping her up into the gurney. The Blue grabbed the knife out of her hand, tossing it into the gutter, believing she was now disarmed. Within seconds, the knife was swiped up by a passerby to save for their next desperate rage-out.

Sasha's agony chilled to a droning growl, her teeth-clenched as they carried her – running, because they *cared* – bursting open the doors of the Tower into a shameful lobby filled with bandaged human wreckage, fresh out of the operating room, all boasting unique bionic limbs, each patient proudly comparing their new appendages. It was a small miracle it was only limbs the Skatterfiends self-mutilated – the technology of the Tower hadn't quite caught up to mechanically simulating vital organs, lucky for all. Evolution was stuck, but managed to work within its limitations, for now.

They assigned her a room immediately, just missing the late Friday night rush. Blue bandaged her swiftly while Red applied a tourniquet on top of the tight gauze. They exited the room, alerting the surgeon she was ready. Sasha counted to ten, got out of the gurney, and opened the door.

She looked both ways.

Coast clear.

She turned right down the hall, hobbling to the end, then turned right again. Her memory served. She saw that unmarked door to the rarely used stairs.

She began her ascent. She started her cruel, un-ergonomic pattern – throwing her wounded leg up over three sets of stairs, before pulling the rest of herself up. Her groan took on new octaves with each flight achieved, the Demerol now an antiquated shadow of itself, a joke. Her psyche sunk as she climbed, only brief repose found in clutching the machete still in her back-sheath, reminding herself what she was doing, who she was going to do it to. She could smell him. Unabashed woman's intuition now told her he was in the same office.

She had counted twenty-four flights. She had ten more to go. She threw her leg up on flight twenty-five and kept at it. She dissociated. She did it well.

Experience.

The door to the thirty-fourth floor emerged out of Sasha's suffocating horizon as she reached the top of her last flight, giving her shuddering waves of nausea that only nostalgia can bring when the drugs wear off. She reached behind her, gripping the machete tight as she slowly brought it out, relishing the smooth scraping sound of its removal to distract her from the worry of what could be on the other side of that door. She turned the knob and kicked it open.

Nothing. Her once bustling floor was now deserted in eerie silence. All trash receptacles and gaudy paintings on the wall gone, leaving nothing but off-white walls boasting an aimless institutional dread. Like a dream of a familiar place, though not as you left it. The dead-air, the non-activity nearly paralyzed Sasha in anticipatory panic, but she continued down the hall, sword drawn, to the door of her old office, down there on the left.

CRIMSON IT, LLC the door read.

She took a deep breath, the first one she recalled taking since she brought down the blade on herself. She turned the knob. Unlocked, she opened it just enough to get a cracking glimpse.

She saw the back of him, in front of a computer monitor, a solitary desk in the middle of an empty room. Gone was her cubicle. Gone were her co-workers. Gone was any kind of hustle and bustle besides the silent buzz of this compromised version of Forrest Griffin; her one-time chivalrous sponsor who got her off the streets, off rock cocaine, helped her hone her knack for numbers, then gave her a data-programming job at CRIMSON IT where she excelled faster than anyone with a stable address. He was her boss; she was his living, breathing *project* – until one day she got her papers to walk, no accountability from Griffin. How could there be, when he simply disappeared?

Until now. This nearly comedic sight of his freakish, hunchbacked form – his once perfectly coifed curly hair had grown to the uneven length of an 80s stand-up comedian.

Still just peeking through the cracked door, she noticed an oxygen tank to his side, tubes leading to his still un-revealed front.

She swung the door wide, strong.

It hit the wall.

Forrest jerked his head around at the sound, revealing the grotesque sight of his expressionless face, now dominated by a gapping metal frame around the hole that was once his mouth. A charred black crater now, illuminated only by remnants of teeth blown to mere nubs, like sucked-on Tic-Tacs, crude wiring sewn into his lips attached to the thin steel mounting to keep this festering void permanently open; it no longer functioned as God intended since his accident.

He saw her machete drawn, lit up by her dagger eyes. Unable to speak a coherent language, he creaked out a pathetic groan of terror, his denial expiring. He thought he'd never see her again.

She heard it as "have mercy, please." Exhausted by the intolerable sight of this imperiled version of Griffin, Sasha lowered her sword. Her adrenaline subsided, slowly dissipating to curious pity. It was clear someone or something had already taught him a barbarous lesson.

He motioned her over in a panic, opening a Word program to communicate. Solemnly, she mustered the courage to walk over while he frantically pointed to the screen as he began to type:

<*You have every right to be upset with me but please allow me to explain. It may seem like I abandoned you, but I abandoned everyone – the Indonesian company QUE took over and I was forced to fire one person a day until there was no one left, so there wouldn't be an uprising. I picked you first to get the hardest part over with first. You were all replaced by scab imports who already knew the pharma-robotics business. QUE's takeover of the tower happened very quickly. I had no*

say in what was happening. In fact, I haven't been outside of the tower in over a year. I am trapped here>

Forrest lifted his pant leg up to reveal a black ankle brace with a flashing red light, his tracking device if he should attempt to exit the tower.

<When they took over, I was forced to turn CRIMSON IT into an automaton farm of employees who would coordinate shipping of Skatter throughout the world. The stress of the job led to a nervous breakdown, after which they didn't know what to do with me. They couldn't let me out of the tower with all the inside info I had accrued, and I wanted to stay part of the team, so ironically, I had to relapse. They put me in the TEST branch – one of the classified tiers here, a human guinea pig room where they test the new altered batches to make sure that they're 'safe' in small doses. While they have to keep changing the chemical make-up of Skatter to keep it legal, they also have to change Gather to match the effects. Well, I got a bad batch of Gather that corroded my mouth, the upper part of my throat, and part of my nasal cavity. It was like giving birth through my fucking face, Sasha.>

<Robotics haven't developed a way to replicate these parts of human anatomy yet, so here I am, living proof that we're suspended in this corrupt evolution.>

He backspaced.

<'evolution.' While I wait in vain for the technology to breakthrough, they have me hidden alone in this room where I am now doing menial data entry. No one can see me or else it would be bad publicity for Skatter and the whole enterprise. I am fed through this tube here, and oxygen comes through this one. I sleep in this reclining chair, my last thought every night is that I hope to die peacefully in my sleep.>

In decompressing increments, Sasha felt her anger subside – not without flashes of bewilderment rolling from her head to her weakening knees. A seismic shift of fermented emotion fell slowly from its final form before vengeance could be carried out. She felt dizzy – pain, drugs, insomnia, this curveball development before her – she took a seat next to Forrest as he continued to type his desperate, hopeless alibi. At least she would not kill him.

<Now, the thing is… like any corporate business model, they cut corners in the name of profit. Too many cooks in the kitchen, too much acceleration on the production line, infighting, things fall under the radar. You understand what they do, right? Just the same as they stay ahead of the DEA to keep it legal; when they make a tainted batch, they just slightly alter the formula, then give it to one single person in TEST, not taking into account all the different blood types and physiology out there. We are all different. They haven't even thought that we might be building a resistance to GATHER, like any other antidote or vaccine. So, it's not just the batch that can be tainted – it can be the person, whose defenses are just not as strong. Think of the fact that we know trauma can be passed down through generations of oppressed cultures. It becomes part of their DNA. But there's a theory that cultures like that have built up a resistance to poisonous elements, compared to those who haven't quite been through as much through the ages. Maybe it's my white guilt talking, Sasha, but I have a feeling that's why this happened to me. My privileged pigment might have sealed my own doom, where I am praying for death now. Or something like it.>

***

As Forrest continued typing to Sasha, night had enveloped downtown, street parties in full swing. The SKATTERLIFE caravan rolled hard on their beat after cutting a large swathe of the Friday evening melee. Camera One began setting up shop on the corner of 6th and San Pedro in front of The Midnight Mission, for full-frame vantage of Blameson and Hunter mixing it up with the most authentic Skatter-goers yet. This was the heart of a once contained Skid Row, where people had been doing Skatter the longest; therefore, built up the highest tolerance; therefore, partied the hardest.

The intersection was the nucleus of the new zombie elite, who, ironically, accumulated enough preservation through years of hard living that they had the constitution to always take it to the next level with the drug.

Tolerance.

There was a beat-up drum set outside of the Mission the zonked out would beat on, prompting others to punch aluminum trash cans, anything that would make a deranged poly-rhythmic racket with the beat. The crowds contorted, twisted and shuffled to a writhing din of percussion that sounded like a call to war.

<And Sasha, even when they dispose of a bad batch — they just throw it in the dumpster in back, no biohazard containers or anything, where anyone can just take it. You don't think things have gotten so desperate down there that you street people aren't cutting corners too? Or the Reds and Blues may be selling it to them instead of the trialed batches to double their money?>

"Camera One! You getting this?" Maggie laughed as she pointed at Mark, who was getting his groove on with some black folk high on the block's totem. They were teaching Mark to two-step for starters, to get his feet wet, but those two left feet remained dry, clumsy; guaranteed to be nice slapstick for viewers at home while embarrassing everyone involved. Mark's stubborn, unwieldly perseverance convinced him he was bridging the grand chasm of racial inequality. Camera One pointed at handheld Camera Two to get a closer view.

<I know some bad batch is down there, probably somewhere really close...>

Maggie stood in front of Camera One, staring it down jovially as she began the scene report.

"Well, look at this, folks! Now *this* is a party! We've got drums, we've got fire, we got trash cans, and we have trash cans *as* drums *on* fire! Is there even enough room out there for all these smiles and good vibes? Hell, Mark is finally learning to dance…"

<But you know what really kills me, Sasha?>

Camera One zeroed in on Mark taking another hit from his new dance teacher's pipe, as they laughed, egging him on.

<Is that when this happened to me…>

Mark began to compensate for his tumultuous footwork by picking up speed, screaming, uncontainable. He yanked his tie loose, forehead sweating profusely. He grabbed his blazer tail and peeled it off awkwardly from his backside, tangling himself in his own outfit until he threw it down in front of him, a triumphant matador being internally impaled by his own organs. The crowd cheered, he tore open his button shirt, howling with spilled over Skatter psychosis.

<I'll never know what my face looked like as it was erasing itself…>

"Yo yo yo! Get this man some Gather! Who's got the Gather?" Mark's urban dance coach implored anyone holding within earshot.

A solemn-eyed but determined Mexican man heeded the call, running up with a baggie of antidote. Mark, too winded and adrenaline-sick to save himself. His hands, busy, confused, unable to cease clawing at his skin, searching his pockets like looking for keys to a way out of it.

<All I know is what their faces looked like...>

The Mexican man tried calming Mark with kind words while prying his mouth open, administering the life-saving paste under his trembling tongue. Upon contact, the paste began to foam up. Mark gagged trying to spit it out, but it was too late. He screamed for good reason now, foam corroding his showbiz teeth, all that was underneath, his lips melting into indistinguishable blood-dribble.

"Bad batch, man."

Maggie pointed at Camera One and Camera Two to make sure they were getting all of it, honing all her acting skills into one compressed effort as she internalized her ecstasy, knowing how good the ratings were going to be.

<Looking back at me
In absolute horror.>

Acknowledgements

Enormous gratitude to Craig Douglas and everyone else at Close to the Bone for their patience, drive, and zero-bullshit professionalism.

Much obliged to author/poet Jean-Paul Garnier (of Space Cowboy Books/Simultaneous Times podcast) who not only gave a home to some of my earliest short stories but also introduced me to the mad joy of editing. That part of the process is now my favorite part of writing since it requires the most cognition, therefore you're more conscious to enjoy it. The rough draft is always just such a blur of 'what just happened?' as opposed to editing, where you actually get to figure it out.

Others to thank for first dibs: Black Hare Press, John Bowie at Bristol Noir, Ron Earl and Paul Garth at Shotgun Honey, Alec Cizec at Pulp Modern, Ron and Deidre at Mannison Press, Manuel Marrero at Expat Press, Ted Prokash at Joyless House, Stuart Buck at Bear Creek Gazette, Francis Moss at Desert Writer's Guild, the wicked pen and fine taste of Van Rijn, Todd at 10th Rule Books, Louise Zedda-Sampson and Chris Mason at Things in the Well.

An honor to receive the kind and sincere words from Chandler Morrison, Chris Kelso, William R Soldan and again to Manuel Marrero; as well as Michael T. Fournier (Razorcake), J.B. Stevens (EconoClash Review) and to my cousin Katherine Murphy from Artful Efforts.

Special thanks to Steven J. Golds for the encouragement to pursue this project.

About the Author

Gabriel Hart is the author of *Virgins in Reverse/The Intrusion, A Return to Spring*, and the forthcoming novel *The Devils of Blackout Beach*. His book of poetry *UNSONGS Vol. 1* was released by Close to The Bone in 2021. He's a monthly columnist for *Lit Reactor*, *EconoClash Review*, and a regular contributor to *Los Angeles Review of Books*. His punk Wall of Sound group Jail Weddings are currently working on the follow-up to their 2019 album *Wilted Eden*. He lives in California's High Desert.

Made in United States
North Haven, CT
04 November 2021

10844700R00109